TWELVE

By David Farrell

Also By David Farrell

The Last Resort

The Glove

You Can't Get Rid of Me That Easily

Printed in Australia
First Printing 2019

Paperback ISBN 978-1-644-67838-1

Dedicated with love

To Our Collection.

x x x

CONTENTS

I WORK OUT   1

ALWAYS   9

WHATEVER IT TAKES   21

THE LEADING MAN   31

TO WHOM IT MAY CONCERN   43

DON'T WANT TO MISS A THING   55

FORTUNE TELLER   67

AFTER THE MOVIE   73

VHS   93

COMPANION   101

STRANGE   109

THE AIRPORT   123

I WORK OUT

'You have to lose weight Mr Cortez.'

'You're right Doc. I'm not getting the roles I want because of my size.'

'It's not *just* that Donald. You're looking a bit…unhealthy.'

Donnie Cortez didn't like the way his doctor said the word *unhealthy*. He felt for the first time in a long time that he was being judged. As an actor working in Los Angeles he knew that appearances were important – sometimes the *most* important thing. It wasn't about what role you were actually involved in so much as speculation about what you might do next. Donnie used to be in amazing shape. He'd played a gladiator in a sword and sandal picture where he'd been shirtless in almost every scene. The roles had been drying up lately and Donnie – now aged thirty-eight – had been struggling with maintaining any kind of exercise regime.

'Listen Doc… I have gained a few…but I'm healthy aren't I? I mean…I'm not going to have a heart attack, right?'

'Losing weight is a preventative tactic Mr Cortez. You might not have any immediate health concerns but they *will* develop. You are approaching a dangerous age. Risks increase as you get older and you'll need to be more responsible about your weight.'

'So what do you want me to do?'

'There are apps you could download. Do you have a Fitbit Mr Cortez?' the doctor enquired.

'Nah. I don't *do* technology. I'm old school!'

'Very well…perhaps something old school then.'

The doctor dug through his desk drawer and pulled out a basic pedometer.

'Take this. I want you to start with a goal of ten thousand steps a day. That translates to about five miles. Do you think you can walk five miles a day?'

'Sure. I probably already walk *ten* miles a day!' he boasted.

'That's good. This will measure it for you. Just clip it to your belt.'

'Hmmm… I guess I could do that.' Donnie was suddenly worried that he would fail at this task. He didn't like to fail.

Donnie felt challenged by the current state of technology. Upcoming actors were gaining an online presence through podcasting, twitter and vlogs. He didn't know where to begin. To make matters worse the number of followers people had was now a factor for casting agents. People thought programs would perform better if they had an instant audience. Shows were expecting talent to bring viewers to the party through social media. Donnie's agent had offered to set up and maintain some online accounts for him but he had declined the offer over a year ago and was too proud to ask for help now.

Donnie clipped the pedometer to his belt and walked around the room. It seemed to work just fine. With each step Donnie took the pedometer dutifully added a number to its count.

He left the office and started to walk downtown. Lunchtime was approaching and Donnie had planned on getting a pastrami sandwich at *The Deli on the Corner*. Now – after the doctor's appointment – he was having second thoughts. He loved those sandwiches. They had melted cheese and far too much meat.

Nobody else made sandwiches like that around here. LA was full of health freaks that were always on a new fad diet.

When he reached *The Deli* he paused in the window. Theresa was working at the counter. Donnie had always liked Theresa. She was short but very buxom. He liked to steal a look at her chest when she was concentrating and weighing meat on the scales. Donnie had been dating a woman from New York named Zara for a couple of months. She had come out to LA for pilot season and decided to stay and try her luck. She was cute but she was no Theresa. He knew so little about this woman but lusted after her all the same.

As he was standing outside the Deli a couple of teenagers asked him for a photo. Donnie obliged posing with each of them individually. They were pleasant enough and he loved being recognised. They immediately posted the picture on social media and tagged Donnie's location for the world to see. He remained blissfully unaware. He discreetly checked the pedometer and found that it sat at just over two thousand steps. Maybe this would be easier than he thought!

He went inside and locked eyes with Theresa.

'Hey gorgeous,' she said with a smile that made Donnie melt like cheese.

She was perfect.

'Hi Theresa. How's things?'

'Good thanks. What can I get you today?'

'Pastrami sandwich, extra cheese please.'

'Sure. Twelve dollars Donnie.'

'Thanks.'

Theresa smiled again after she closed the register.

'Look at you… all famous,' she said as she grabbed a hunk of pastrami with her gloved hand.

'Sorry…what do you mean?'

'I saw you posing for pictures with your fans.'

'Oh yeah? You saw that?'

'Yeah!' Theresa sounded impressed.

'That happens sometimes.'

'So when am I going to see your face on one of these magazines?' she asked as she indicated towards a plastic shelf containing the weekly gossip rags.

'Oh I dunno. The paparazzi follow me around sometimes…on a slow day.'

'Nonsense! You're a pretty big deal. You did that movie about the uh… the fisherman!'

'Yeah…I did,' he said with a grin. Donnie had been consistently working for years but he thought – and the critics agreed – that the quality of his work was suffering.

He flirted for a few minutes and then sat in a booth that faced Theresa to eat his lunch. She was always so nice to him that he made sure to leave a healthy tip. He liked her almost as much as the pastrami sandwiches she delivered him so regularly.

The extreme feeling of guilt didn't hit him until his plate was empty. He looked at his bulging stomach and felt ashamed.

How could I have just eaten that? He thought to himself. After I came from that check-up.

He had made the decision without hesitation. Theresa swung her hips as she wiped the glass countertop nearby. She was humming a tune that Donnie didn't recognise.

What now? Is this my life? Do I just keep eating whatever I want until I balloon out into some kind of character actor? That was never the plan!

Donnie decided that he needed a drastic move in order to ensure he would lose weight. He couldn't keep succumbing to temptation. He knew that The Deli was his biggest weakness – as was his infatuation with Theresa. It wasn't good for his waistline or his relationship with Zara for that matter. He decided on the most balls out move he could think of. He would ask out Theresa. When she inevitably said no he would finally have closure and be far too embarrassed to come back into her shop. He shouldn't be dropping by three times a week anyway. It wasn't going to be easy but neither was losing the weight.

You want to be a leading man? This is how you do it. You need the heartbreak and the humiliation Donnie! You need this!

He wanted to act in big budget films and become a movie star. He wanted people to remember the name Donnie Cortez. It was always about the next big move for Donnie. This was a small sacrifice on the road to glory.

'Hey Theresa?'

'Yeah?'

'You and me…we should go out sometime.'

Theresa placed one hand on her hip and threw a tea towel over her shoulder.

'Sure,' she said with a grin. 'I'm free Saturday.'

Shit.

'Saturday huh?'

'Yeah.'

'Alright…good.'

They exchanged numbers and Donnie left *The Deli*. During his Uber ride home he cursed his handsome face and charming personality.

Now I've gotta go on a date with her? And then what? If it goes well then I'll have to dump Zara…and I'll be eating nothing but Pastrami sandwiches every week! Maybe the sex will be better with Theresa but I'll be dead sooner!

When he reached his home it struck him that he hadn't checked his pedometer in hours. He was disappointed to see his lazy day reflected in a numerical value. Had he sat around *that* much? He had barely walked at the doctor's office or *The Deli*. Now he felt guilty again. Inside the house he knew Zara would be waiting. She knew he was going to see the doctor. She deserved to know that he was taking steps – *literal* steps – to improve his health. After all it had been her idea to go in the first place.

He didn't want to go in there and show her such a small number on the pedometer. His goal for the day was ten thousand and he wasn't even close! Donnie took out his keys and sat down in his car. He loved his Mustang and drove it as little as possible. LA was full of crazy drivers and tourists and the car had once belonged to his father. They had restored it together over a two-year period. It was one of the happiest memories of his life. It felt so long ago. Donnie didn't like to think about the fact that his father had died of a heart attack at the age of forty-eight but it kept creeping into his mind.

Tomorrow I'll get up and walk. I'll do the ten thousand steps a day. I'll commit to this for you Dad. I want to grow old! I'll make it to my fifties!

Donnie stroked the steering wheel cover with one hand as he held the pedometer in the other. Out of the corner of his eye he noticed that it clicked over with the flick of his wrist. He jostled it a few more times and enjoyed seeing the numbers dance ahead.

Donnie lowered the pedometer out of sight and gave it a gentle shake. He could see the light on in the kitchen. Zara was making dinner for them both. It would probably include a healthy portion of steamed vegetables. Suddenly he was glad that he had eaten the sandwich. He shook the pedometer more and more furiously. There was a feeling that he was getting away with something now. He decided he would lead Zara to believe he was home late because he was out walking. He would enjoy a night of passion before he ended things with her.

This would be his final duplicitous act before he turned everything around. Maybe he and Theresa were destined for bigger things. Maybe he would settle down with her. Theresa seemed to admire him despite his decline in work. Despite his physique. Maybe she would inspire something in him.

Theresa could be my muse.

When he reached ten thousand steps on the pedometer he stopped. He opened the car door, walked up the driveway and went inside his house. Zara had indeed cooked up steamed vegetables with tuna on the side. They talked about his day and he showed off his step count. She made love to him that night.

The next morning Donnie slept in.

A photographer named Dale Davis had been near *The Deli* the day before. He'd seen the photos that Donnie had taken with the teenagers and decided to check it out. In his mind Donnie was all washed up.

Dale was hoping to get some candid photos that showed how fat he'd gotten between acting jobs. The photographer used his van as a hiding place and snapped lots of pictures of Donnie ogling Theresa. He captured in great detail the sloppy manner in which Donnie devoured his pastrami sandwich. He followed him home and – to his amazement - caught Donnie in what appeared to be an act of self-gratification in his Mustang.

Dale couldn't explain why Donnie arrived home that evening only to sit in his vehicle and masturbate but he was thrilled when he did. Dale sold all of his photos to a series of magazines for one of the biggest paydays of his paparazzi life.

Donnie Cortez was famous again.

ALWAYS

'We've only been dating for twelve months! How could you?'

Brad wasn't sure how to respond. It was a fair question but he didn't have a fair answer. He wanted to tell Jenny that he didn't love her anymore but that was an awful thing to say. He wanted to tell her that he had been less sexually attracted to her lately but that was obvious to them both.

'I'm sorry that I've hurt you,' he offered.

Endings are hard.

Jenny cried into her hands. She had felt sure that Brad was the one. She wanted to spend the rest of her life with him.

'You always do this. You are the most selfish human being on the planet! Your mother was right about you.'

'What does my mother have to do with this?'

Brad was genuinely confused.

'Your mother told me you were like this. She called you *immature*. When we went to dinner with her and you left the room she implied I would be better off without you.'

'Oh she *implied* it did she?' mused Brad.

'She said that you would never settle down. Looks like mother knows best!' said Jenny folding her arms.

The café was crowded and although Jenny didn't want to make a scene she felt like screaming at the top of her lungs.

'I'm not immature. I'm just nostalgic. I still like the same things that I did when I was a kid.'

'You'd rather watch Professional Wrestling than make love to me,' seethed Jenny. She could feel herself turning red in the face.

'Oh that's rubbish,' he protested. 'You're remembering things wrong.'

'Are you gay? It's alright if you are… just tell me.'

'You think I'm gay because I watch *wrestling*?' asked Brad.

'Well… maybe. Do you like it because it involves greased up men embracing each other?'

'No! I like it because it's like a soap opera. They have… storylines…oh you wouldn't understand!'

'I suppose not!' Jenny was livid. She leaned in and spoke softly so that no one else around them could hear. 'Was it the sex?'

'What do you mean?'

'Was I… you know… bad at it?'

'No. The sex was fine.'

'Just *fine*?'

'What do you want me to say?' he asked picking up a menu.

'I want you to tell me the truth! Aren't you attracted to me anymore?'

It was a loaded question. If he *was* still attracted to her then why was he breaking up with her? If he wasn't then Jenny would launch into a new set of enquiry about exactly what had changed between them.

'You're a beautiful woman. I just don't think we should be together anymore.'

'That's a cop out.'

'Is it?'

'Yes. I thought we were fine…'

'Just *fine*?' he said with a grin. Brac was thrilled to have an opportunity to throw her words back at her.

'You know what I mean.' She leaned in again. 'We had sex two nights ago.'

'So?'

'So what's changed since then?'

'Nothing.'

'Really? Nothing Brad?'

'Nothing's changed.'

'So what you're telling me is that you wanted to break up with me two days ago but you had sex with me anyway?'

It was becoming harder to suppress her rage. Jenny picked up a menu and hid behind it.

Brad considered this for a moment. To him the act of sex wasn't necessarily tied to how he felt about a person. It was an activity that he felt confident he could perform even if he felt hatred for a woman. He hadn't connected the act of intercourse with anything beyond a physical act. He certainly didn't need to be in love with Jenny to enjoy having sex with her.

'The sex isn't the problem,' he started, 'everything else is. I don't feel like we are moving towards anything.'

'So you don't…' she trailed off.

'I don't what?'

'You don't love me?'

'I'm sorry.'

It wasn't what Jenny wanted to hear. If he loved her, which she had no reason to believe as he had never expressed it during their relationship, then maybe this was salvageable. Brad didn't love her and therefore it was over.

'So that's it then? We aren't going to move in together?'

'No.'

'And we're not going to your brother's wedding in May?'

'No.'

'And everything I bought you for your birthday?'

'What did you buy me for my birthday?' he asked. Brad was genuinely curious, as they had started dating just before his birthday last year. They had agreed at the time that a present wasn't required as their relationship was so new. He wondered what she had gleaned from the past year and how her new perspective had manifested itself in gift form.

'You'll never know now!' she snapped back at him.

A waitress came to their table and took their orders. Neither party wanted to make a scene of their break up and both found themselves quite hungry. Without words they seemed to agree to a kind of last supper together.

'So... is there someone else?' she asked.

'No. There's no one else.'

'But there will be,' she said in a disappointed tone.

'Well...yeah maybe one day.'

'And you'll compare me to her,' she said with a sigh.

'It's possible. But… I mean… it wasn't *all* bad. We had some good times too.'

Brad thought of their year of sex and the many semi-public places where they had given in to their urges.

Jenny thought about the time Brad came over during a thunderstorm to check on her and the nature walk they went on during a weekend away.

'There is so much I love about you Brad. You're an amazing guy.'

'Thank you.'

'I want you to be happy. It's just.. '

'You thought we'd stay together? he said quickly.

'Yeah. I thought we were both happy already.'

Brad placed his hands over the top of her hands on the table. Jenny was frozen with anticipation.

Have I changed his mind?

'We don't really like the same things. We like each other – sure – but we don't want to spend time together do we?' Brad removed his hands from hers.

'What do you mean? We're together every weekend!'

'But whenever I'm with you I kind of wish I was doing… something else.'

'More like *someone* else.'

'It's not like that. You don't like me. You like having a boyfriend.'

'That's not true!'

13

'It is. All of your friends have boyfriends. They all share photos with their boyfriends on social media. You're always trying to make me go out somewhere stupid and pose for those fake pictures with you.'

'I'm trying to be cultured!' Jenny folded her arms.

'You're trying to make it seem like we are happier than we are. We're kind of happy but I feel like we're just going through the motions. Don't you think there is some handsome guy out there that would actually *enjoy* posing near a waterfall with you?'

'That's not the point. You don't even want to try!'

She could feel tears forming in her eyes. She didn't want to admit that Brad might be right. She didn't want to confess that she had her doubts about their relationship. Jenny wanted to be as happy as her profile picture made her seem.

'I've been trying. Dating you has barely evolved in the time we have been together. Like, for example, what do you want to do with your life? What are your goals?'

'What do you mean?'

'Well Jen you have a Bachelor of Arts degree now but you're still working at a fast food place. What's next for you? What do you want?'

'Well… I thought about getting married and having a family.'

'And you wanted that with me?'

'Yes! Of course I did!'

'I'm not ready to get married.'

'I know Brad. Your mother told me so.'

'This has got nothing to do with my mother! If you were the right girl I would marry you but you aren't so I don't want to!'

'Oh I'm not the right girl?'

'No!'

'Why not?'

'I don't know…you don't inspire me. I don't want to see you every day. I don't think you're ready to be a wife or a mother… lots of reasons!'

'I don't *inspire* you?

'No you don't.'

Jenny paused dramatically. Her mouth hung open like a broken suitcase.

'And what *does* inspire you?'

'I don't know yet. I just know it isn't you.'

Jenny let a wave of emotion wash over her.

'That really hurts Brad,' she said in a shaky voice.

Brad furrowed his brow and leaned in even closer.

'Wouldn't you rather know now? I don't want to waste your time,' he implored.

'It just feels like we've hardly even started.'

'We've seen each other every weekend for a year. We don't really talk on the phone. Its just sex isn't it? When you boil it all down?'

'It's not just sex!' she protested. 'This was special.'

'Lately you've just been coming over and we've been hooking up.'

'So?'

'So Jenny…we're not talking. You're not staying over.'

The waitress came by and dropped loaded plates in front of them. They both started eating immediately.

Brad studied Jenny's face as he hurled a French fry into his mouth. She was still young and beautiful but she was only interesting on the surface. There was nothing behind her green eyes.

'I feel like… I just feel like I've already wasted my time.'

'It's not a waste if you learn something from it,' he said as he poured tomato sauce onto his plate.

'Did you learn something from this year with me?' she asked innocently.

I learned what I didn't want.

'I suppose so.'

'What?'

'I guess I learned that I need to get out there more. I need to leave the house and do more things. You showed me that there is a whole world going on that I…I guess I want to be a part of.'

'Just not with me?'

'We aren't suited to each other at all.'

'But maybe I could try and watch wrestling with you. And you could visit me at work more. Maybe we can read a book together or take a holiday.'

'Jen, those are all great ideas but it's too late.'

'It's not too late!'

'We need to just stop this. I'm not happy.'

The waitress came back and hovered for a moment at their table. Sensing the awkward nature of their date she wisely moved on.

'Maybe you're right. I just don't want to go through the whole…meeting people and starting dating again.'

'But that's the only way you'll find the person that you're meant to be with. A person that makes you happy every day.'

'Do you really believe in all that? I've never heard you talk about this kind of thing before.'

'Of course I do. My parents have been together over thirty-five years. I want that kind of relationship too.'

'I think if that's what you're looking for then you're probably right. The idea of being with someone for thirty-five years scares me.'

'You should just think of it one day at a time. Thirty-five years don't just happen. You *build* a relationship by wanting the same things and having the same values. Then you are having so much fun that suddenly it's been thirty-five years.'

'You're pretty smart aren't you Brad?'

'I like to think so.'

Jenny finally gave in to her emotions and started to cry, her lips quivering uncontrollably.

'It's so sad,' she managed to say between sobs. 'That it's over.'

'It's only going to get better Jen.'

'Do you promise?'

'I promise.'

They heard screams from across the room first. Neither of them knew quite what was happening until the wave of terror and confusion was too close to ignore. A man wearing a balaclava was poised at the café window with an automatic rifle in hand. He sprayed bullets into the crowd of patrons as Jenny slid beneath the table in fear.

'Oh my God!'

People fell to the tiled floor like rag dolls. Blood splattered and somewhere towards the kitchen a stack of plates shattered as it crashed against the floor. Jenny looked over at Brad who had collapsed next to her beneath the table. He'd been shot three times in the chest and was struggling to apply any kind of pressure to the wounds.

'Brad? Oh my God....BRAD!' she screamed.

The masked man moved towards the back of the café and continued to fire.

She wished that she knew what to do but she didn't. Jenny tried to pull him towards her but he was too heavy to move.

'Brad...hang in there.'

He jerked his head in pain. His eyes looked down at his chest and then back at Jenny. Brad smiled and accepted his fate. She could sense he was giving up. She slapped his face and tried to keep him there with her.

'Stay with me Brad, okay? It's almost your birthday. Did you want to know what I bought you? I bought you an authentic Mexican wrestling mask.'

Brad smiled and then closed him eyes for the final time.

Jenny screamed. She'd never felt a more overwhelming pain or sorrow in her entire life. She'd never experienced the death of a loved one before this moment. Saliva fell from her mouth freely.

Her cries drew the attention of the shooter who doubled back to find her smeared with Brad's blood. He held out his gun with a fully outstretched arm and pointed the barrel at her. Without a second thought the shooter put Jenny out of her newfound misery.

In the aftermath the two were remembered lovingly by friends, co-workers and family members.

Nobody knew that they were at all unhappy and they were mourned as a couple struck down in the early stages of their relationship.

WHATEVER IT TAKES

When she was thirty-four years young Trudy noticed a hot new trend: All of her friends were getting pregnant. It was an epidemic – just as *getting married* had been two years before. Her friends were glowing as one by one they announced their little miracles on their social media profiles.

LIKE.

LIKE.

LIKE.

LIKE.

Should I become a mother too? Trudy wondered. Her husband Roy had always wanted children but it had never seemed trendy enough for her. She wasn't about to throw caution to the wind and be the first! Now that enough other people in her social circles were getting pregnant Trudy thought the timing might be right. Roy was gainfully employed at a metal factory and their marriage was back on solid ground. It had been a rough patch for them when affairs were in vogue but they'd worked it out. And that was months ago anyway!

Trudy didn't want to be left behind. After some wine she decided to have unprotected sex with her husband. When her period came later that month she took her disappointment out on Roy. When two more months passed she questioned his abilities as a man. Roy was exceedingly average in every way. Trudy took vitamins and scheduled sex with him every night. Her husband just wanted to relax and watch television but Trudy wouldn't take no for an answer. She insisted that their marriage and social standing depended on it.

'Don't you love me Roy?'

He did…and so he made love to his wife again and again until he had nothing left to give.

She elevated her pelvis when he was done and scrolled through her friend's latest posts.

LIKE.

LIKE.

LIKE.

LIKE.

After five months of trying Trudy was ready to throw in the towel. What was the point? If she couldn't get pregnant soon her children would be too far apart in age to be in the same classes as her friend's children. *My friends and I will drift apart too* she thought to herself. Roy was no help at all. He kept offering to cook and clean and massage her. He was utterly useless to Trudy.

It was a pop up Internet ad that suggested the specialist.

On the computer screen an animated sperm raced towards a smiling egg. They collided and, after an explosion cleared, a baby looked back at her. The image alone was almost enough to bring Trudy to tears.

She made an appointment and the next day Trudy found herself at a residence just one suburb over. The sign on the mailbox said *Pregnancy Expert Max Wallflower.*

She followed a path around the house to a freestanding caravan in the backyard. Its tyres were flat and the grass around it looked overgrown. Trudy knocked on the white door.

'Hello?'

A man with shoulder length brown hair and a goatee opened the door. He wasn't wearing a shirt and Trudy was drawn to the mystical symbols that he'd had tattooed on his pectoral muscle. She didn't know what they meant.

'You must be Trudy,' he said in a low voice. 'Welcome. I'm Max.'

Max led Trudy into the caravan where she sat down on the only available surface – a queen sized bed. It was too large for the space and Max explained that it had been delivered in a compressed state and had expanded after opening.

'I understand you are having some trouble getting pregnant,' he said sympathetically.

Trudy showed Max her friend's social media posts and explained her fears about missing out. She told him how she saw the pop up advertisement and the circumstances that led her to seek out his services.

'Do you think you'll be able to help?' she asked.

Max stroked his goatee before answering.

'I can see that your intentions are pure. I can help you but you must do one thing for me.'

'Anything,' replied Trudy.

'You must believe.'

Trudy nodded. She was willing to do anything.

'Alright doctor.'

'I'm not a doctor. Unless you *believe* I am.'

'Um...okay,' she replied quickly. He loomed large, as he stood barefoot in front of her.

'Alright then, we shall begin. I promise you will fall pregnant Trudy. My methods have been called unorthodox but they certainly get results. I've never failed.'

This was promising news and Trudy couldn't help but smile.

'So how many women have you helped to become pregnant Mr Wallflower?'

'Please – call me Max. I have helped two women so far.'

'Oh.'

'Are you ready to be the third?'

Trudy imagined posting images of herself online with a pregnant belly. She loved the idea.

'I am.'

Max asked her to lie down on the bed and she did. It was very comfortable. He asked her to remove her pants and underwear. She complied once again. Trudy felt a little bit strange as she lay half naked on the bed but did her best to 'believe' this was the answer.

'Trudy…what I am about to ask you is the strangest part of this process. I need you to consent to intercourse…here and now…with me.'

'Intercourse? Like sex?'

'Yes Trudy,' he replied. 'I will remove my pants and insert myself into you. It is through this process that your body will become ready to receive a baby.'

Trudy imagined joining a mother's group and discussing breastfeeding on a forum.

'Alright. I'm ready.'

Max removed his jeans and stood in front of Trudy. He was already aroused.

What a professional!

He gently knelt down and applied lubricant, first onto Trudy and then onto himself. He lay down on top of Trudy and inserted himself into her in a rehearsed motion.

'Oh,' she said as she felt her body accepting him. 'That's great.'

'You're doing very well Trudy. Very well indeed,' he said between thrusts.

Trudy kept her hands by her sides but had the urge to touch his arms and chest. The process felt liberating.

'Do you want to get pregnant?' he asked her.

'Yes.'

'Louder Trudy!'

'YES!'

'Do you *believe*?'

'Yes. Yes. Yes. YES!'

Max came inside her. After a moment of pause he climbed off, cleaned up and put his jeans back on one leg at a time.

'Now Trudy... this is the important part... I want you to go home and have sex with your husband tonight. You might like to do it in exactly the same way we did here today.'

'Tonight? Sure, I can do that.' She sat up on the bed.

'Your body is ready to receive a child. I felt it. I want you to come back on Friday and we'll repeat the process, alright?'

'Friday should be fine. And I should plan on having sex with my husband on Friday night too?' Trudy asked as she started to dress herself again.

Max nodded softly and stroked his goatee.

'Yes please. You should be having sex with him after each of our sessions.'

Max opened an unmarked bottle and poured out four small yellow pills.

'Take one of these now and one each day until Friday. I'll provide you with more then.'

'What are they?' she asked holding one between her fingers.

'I call them *Fertility Boosters*. They should help your body during this phase of growth.'

She took a bottle of water from her bag and swallowed one of the pills immediately. Max smiled at her as she gulped down the liquid.

'Remember Trudy; the most important part of becoming a mother is to *believe*. I believe in you too. Well done today.'

'Thank you. What do I owe you?'

Max produced a pamphlet and handed it to her. It wasn't a cheap process.

'I don't require any payment from you now. We can work it all out after you're pregnant.'

'I can't wait,' she beamed.

That night she had sex with Roy. For the entire twelve-minute duration she kept repeating a mantra in her head.

Believe.

Believe.

Believe.

Believe.

It was working. Trudy was starting to bel eve. She imagined her friends liking her social media posts. She imagined strangers wanting to rub her belly. She knew that her child would go to school and be in the same year as her friend's children. This would ensure they would all remain in each other's lives and she would stay relevant.

On Friday she returned to the caravan for her second appointment. She disrobed and assurred the position on the mattress.

'Actually Trudy…this time I will require you to present yourself slightly differently.'

At his request Trudy lay on her stomach and pushed her bottom into the air. She splayed her legs apart and Max Wallflower took her from behind. He held her hips gently as he bounced their bodies together rhythmically.

Once again Max asked her questions as he performed his unorthodox process.

'Do you want to get pregnant?' he asked her. Max was grunting significantly more this time around.

'Yes I do.'

'Do you believe you will get pregnant Trudy?'

Trudy pulled a stray hair out of her face and bit her lip in ecstasy.

'YES! OH *YES!*'

On this occasion they climaxed at the same time much to Trudy's surprise. She was embarrassed but Max insisted that this was a good thing.

'It means that it's working.'

'That's good,' Trudy said, collapsing onto the bed.

She was given another set of pills and went home to her husband. Even though she felt sexually satisfied she allowed Roy to mount her that night in a similar fashion.

The third time she visited Max Wallflower he asked her if she wouldn't mind assuming a more dominant role in the process. Trudy agreed to be on top of Max.

'It would also be helpful…to you…if you would remove all of your clothing this time. Being completely nude will help you freely accept that you are ready to be a mother.'

Trudy was more than happy to remove her clothing. It seemed to be a perfectly reasonable request considering Max had been completely naked during each of their previous sessions together.

When they were both undressed she climbed onto him and he inserted himself into her once again. Trudy noted that they didn't need lubricant this time.

Max nodded at her and she started to grind against him. She closed her eyes and continued her mantra.

Believe.

Believe.

Believe.

Believe.

Her concentration was broken when she felt Max grab her buttocks tightly with both hands. She opened her eyes and watched him climax. They stayed locked together for another minute as Max spoke.

'You're a beautiful woman Trudy. Remember to have intercourse with your husband tonight as it is *imperative* to the process.'

'I will.'

'Thank you for your commitment Trudy. You're doing a great job.'

That night she assumed the same dominant position with Roy. She opted for complete nudity in order to repeat the process as closely as possible. She even asked Roy to grab her buttocks when he was about to come. Her husband happily complied.

That week Trudy's period was late.

Had the process been successful already? After only *three* visits?

A pregnancy test confirmed it. She was with child.

Trudy posted a picture of her pregnancy test onto social media the minute she saw that it was positive.

LIKE.

LIKE.

LIKE.

LIKE.

Roy will be thrilled when I tell him tonight she thought to herself with a smile.

When she returned to inform Max of her good fortune the caravan had been removed from the property.

Trudy felt a wave of misery wash over her because now she would never hear the kind words of praise that Max would have surely heaped onto her at this achievement. The love of strangers online would have to suffice for now.

She felt sure that she would be able to procure a similar fertility service when her friends were ready to have their subsequent babies in the years to come. If Roy wasn't up to the task.

As her phone continued to *ping* she placed her hands onto her stomach and imagined the lifetime of milestones that her baby would provide for her and the endless stream of attention she would get on each of her social media platforms.

THE LEADING MAN

'Would you mind taking your shirt off for us Eddie?'

'Sure, no problem.'

Eddie was nervous but he'd never let them see it. He'd been making his living as an actor for more than ten years. Auditions like this didn't bother him anymore. He'd had a moment of clarity that had stayed with him. The less the casting directors and producers thought he wanted the role the more they seemed to want to put him in it. He had the roguish looks of a bad boy and had enjoyed a healthy run playing villains in romantic comedies. Eddie was the guy that women were inexplicably with, before realising they should be with the romantic lead.

He had never thought about being typecast before last month when he was punched in the face at a bar. People had started to assume he and the characters he played were one and the same. It was time to change that.

Eddie was going to be an action star.

He removed his shirt and smiled at the camera that was recording the audition. He'd recently had his teeth whitened and felt like showing them off. He knew he looked good. A combination of expensive personal trainers, dieticians and therapists had each had a hand in sculpting this façade. He was in the greatest condition of his life.

One of the producers removed his glasses and stroked his chin.

'Would you mind doing a read though again for us Eddie? This time I want you to imagine that a horde of busty women have burst through the door. They are all topless and covered in some kind of body paint. From the top.'

Eddie widened his stance and bounced on the spot slightly.

'Look out behind you Professor!' he yelled as he pointed past the camera.

'Help...save me...' spoke a young female assistant sitting next to the camera. She emphasised no words and had no particular inflection. She clearly didn't know how to act. Eddie didn't let it bother him. He was in the zone.

'Nooooooo!' he cried as he forced genuine tears out of his eyes. Instead of wiping them away he took a step closer to the camera.

'What should we do now?' spoke the assistant evenly.

Eddie took a deep breath and tilted his head in a rehearsed manner.

'We're going to have to fondle our way out.'

He paused dramatically before yelling again and running out of the camera's frame. The producers burst into spontaneous applause.

'Well done Eddie!'

'Fantastic!'

He took a bow and picked up his shirt from the floor.

'We'll be in touch.'

Eddie left the room feeling like the part was his. He visualised his phone ringing and his manager telling him the good news. He imagined promotional posters for the film. *Eddie Durant* as *Chris Piper* in *Explosive Cargo*. He grinned to himself.

He took a drive to the beach and called Missy – the girl he'd been seeing for the past few weeks. She didn't answer. He watched the surfers waxing their boards at the local surf shop.

Eddie was told he had only just missed out on the role of Dan Lewis in the film *November Wave*. If he was going to learn to surf it was going to be for a film. He'd completed a bartending course thanks to a minor role in *The Drinks are on Me* and he'd learned Karate thanks to *FU-GET about it*. California had become a beautiful and colourful experience for Eddie. t was everything he'd hoped for when he moved out from Ohio.

He parked in his allocated spot in the underground carpark beneath his building. He'd always thought that in an emergency, like during an earthquake, that he'd never be able to get his car out of there. It was a poorly thought through carpark with an overly complicated design. He wandered up to the fourth floor by way of the stairs. He liked that most people took the elevator. He felt like he was going through some secret back way that nobody else knew about.

There was a message waiting for him when he got through the front door. He liked coming home and playing answering machine messages instead of carrying a mobile phone around. It was a luxury he had earned. He was a more recognisable face now and people actually wanted to put him in their movies. Filmmakers were willing to wait for him to return their calls.

'Eddie! Stan here. Call me when you get in!'

Stan was his manager. He'd 'discovered' Eddie after a local Ohio toothpaste commercial went National over ten years ago. He'd promised fame and riches beyond compare but was yet to really deliver on either. Eddie lived a comfortable life – one he would never complain about – but he had recently discovered something lurking within himself: Ambition.

Eddie wanted to be big. He wanted all the Hollywood clichés. He wanted a star on the Walk of Fame, award nominations and a supermodel girlfriend.

Most of all he wanted to walk into a room of his peers and be praised for his acting. He'd coasted through his career so far on his looks. He knew that. It was time to put some work into his craft.

Explosive Cargo would act as a stepping-stone. He knew the film had sequel written all over it. Maybe even franchise! Eddie would be asked onto all the talk shows and maybe even grace some magazine covers. Definitely the ones focussed on men and their muscles.

This film will get me noticed. Then I can pick and choose my projects.

He returned his managers call.

'They want you Eddie,' said Stan directly.

'Excellent! So you'll work out the money?' he replied.

'Yes… after you head in tomorrow for one last meeting.'

'What for? I thought you said they wanted me?'

'They do…they just don't know it yet! You're in a very small group of guys they want to come back in. Trust me! You're all good Eddie boy!'

The news annoyed Eddie.

Another hoop to jump through.

His phone rang. It was Missy returning his call. He let it go to voicemail. He went for a jog and tried to put it out of his mind.

This final – and supposedly very casual – meeting was taking place on the studio backlot. Eddie was met by a production assistant and ushered through to a waiting room. This was all very strange to him. Weren't they expecting him? The room was a dressing room with a locker and water cooler against one wall. After a few minutes the production assistant came back and apologised.

'Can I get you anything while you wait?' he asked meekly.

'No I'm fine.'

A short time later he returned and beckoned Eddie to follow him. They went through some more backstage areas and into a darkened studio.

'Have a seat here please.'

Eddie obliged. He sat down on a very comfortable leather seat and squinted into the darkness. The seat he now occupied was positioned between two wooden walls. He couldn't see anything around him. Eddie felt like a contestant on *Perfect Match*.

A spotlight came on to his right and a man in a suit walked out in front of him. In the distance he spotted the familiar red light of a studio camera that signalled a recording was in progress.

'Ladies and Gentlemen,' began the suited man, 'Welcome to the show! Do you ever wish you could cast a movie? Did you ever think that you could do a better job than Hollywood? Now is your chance! Welcome to *The Leading Man*!'

Light spilled into the studio illuminating a crowd of two hundred applauding audience members. It was a sensory overload for Eddie who found himself in a state of shock.

'Do you want to meet our stars?' boomed the host.

The applause intensified. Without warning the wooden walls on either side were pulled back and Eddie saw eleven equally stunned men sitting in matching leather chairs.

'Meet the stars of tomorrow – these twelve are your leading men. But only one will emerge as the lead of this summer's biggest blockbuster – *Explosive Cargo*! There can be only one *Leading Man*!'

Eddie recognised some of the other men in the room. He'd seen them at auditions over the years.

The host went from chair to chair introducing each of the men to the audience. None of them questioned the situation they found themselves in. The cameras were rolling and they didn't want to appear difficult. When the host approached Eddie he clicked into publicity mode automatically.

'Well…I didn't know how much I wanted to win until this very moment. Heck, I didn't know I was *competing* until this very moment!' said Eddie.

The audience laughed.

'This is going to be a great show,' he chuckled. 'Now people at home can weigh in on the films they are paying to see. I'm excited!'

The audience cheered. Eddie was becoming a fan favourite already.

There was something alluring about the experiment that was unfolding before him. Suddenly Eddie wanted to win. The Producer of *Explosive Cargo* was a man named Roland. He was doubling as the Producer of the TV show *The Leading Man*. He gathered all of the actors together at the end of the taping and thanked them for being a part of the experiment. Some of the men had been alerted to this ahead of time. Others were as clueless as Eddie.

'You'll all be paid a weekly allowance for being on the show which we estimate will be filmed over the next ten or so weeks.

During that time we will film scenes for *Explosive Cargo*. The winner's scenes will make it into the final film. This will be huge for your profiles. It's going to be incredible,' said Roland with a sincere smile.

Eddie called Stan as soon as he made it back to his car.

'What the hell Stan! Did you know about this?'

'I had no idea! I've only just heard. If you want me to get you out of it I can...'

'No... They already filmed me. The audience saw me...and laughed at my jokes. I think I should do it. Maybe it will be a good career move.'

'This show could be a spectacular failure Eddie. It's uncharted waters.'

'I'll do it.'

When *The Leading Man* aired that Sunday night it was a bonafide hit. All twelve of the men were profiled in print and online media. Betting companies put odds on their success and the studio increased security around the production.

When Eddie turned up for filming he was handed a short seven-page script. The scene involved the lead character Chris Piper and the leading lady trying – and succeeding - to diffuse a bomb.

He went through make up and wardrobe before arriving on the set just in time to see one of the other actors finishing his version of the scene. He seemed to be doing a good job. Eddie didn't need to be reminded that this was a competition.

He worked through the blocking of the scene while cameras recorded his every move for the reality TV show. He played up to the cameras, grinning and showing his white teeth. He tried to channel the persona of an action hero. He wiped his brow as he fumbled to cut the red wire on the bomb. He got lost in the scene.

Eddie had no idea what to expect when he turned up for the next live show. He was surprised to find audience members were dressed in the outfit of Chris Piper – jeans, a white singlet and black leather jacket – and fans had made their own signs. It was much louder than last time too.

One by one their scenes were played on a big screen in the studio. Each actor brought subtle differences to their performance and the audience were asked to assess and vote for their favourite. Another actor – Hunter – was eliminated.

Stan was furiously trying to control the new level of interest in Eddie. He was reviewing scripts that were pouring in every day. Everyone wanted to be in business with *The Leading Man* – whoever that turned out to be. The show was sold to sixty other countries and international versions commenced production.

Eddie started each week by visualising himself as the eventual winner. He dumped Missy and increased his gym regime. Missy wound up doing a 'tell all' about him that was aired during the News but gained little traction.

When there were only seven actors left the show started to bring in action stars of the past to film cameos in *Explosive Cargo*. The show was so popular that none of them could refuse. Eddie coasted through to the top four.

The script for the film was leaked online so production took a week off while the writers rewrote the end of the movie. With so many lucrative sponsorship deals attached to the show and the film they had no trouble adding expensive new stunts and CGI to *Explosive Cargo*. It was now a $200 million dollar behemoth.

Eddie found himself alone with one of the Producers on the set during some down time. The Producer was extremely happy with *The Leading Man* and the overnight success that it – and he – had become.

'It's been really so incredible Eddie… You've been such a big part of it too. I hope you win. I truly do '

'You're so kind,' replied Eddie. 'I hope whoever wins makes *Explosive Cargo* into the best film it can be.'

'It's already been presold to international markets – it's basically made its budget back and we haven't even finished filming! I'd say it's been beyond successful.'

'I'm just happy to be here,' Eddie replied diplomatically.

Media outlets continued to pour through the lives of the final four actors looking for dirt. They sifted through their garbage and spoke to everyone that had ever claimed to have met them.

A company eventually hacked into their personal computers and found pictures of Trevor – considered by most bookies to be an outside chance of winning – in ladies clothing. Trevor had to make a statement about the circumstances that surrounded the photos even though they were taken almost a decade ago.

'It was a Bachelor Party…and I had been drinking,' he began. 'I was dared to wear the clothes and I regret that I allowed these pictures to be taken. It was meant to be some harmless fun.'

When people realised they could make money out of Trevor's past a series of nude photographs surfaced and he was forced out of contention for *The Leading Man.*

Nina Place was the actress they had cast to play Chris Piper's love interest in the film. She had joked many times in print that she was glad that this series was *The Leading Man* and not *The*

Leading Lady or she might not have a job. Nina had been acting, running, fighting and laughing with twelve hopeful actors for weeks. Now that there were only three men left, the media were looking for stories wherever they could find them. Nina was accosted in the carpark by a camera crew and asked who she thought would win the show.

'Eddie Durant, maybe. I think he could do well.'

It was an innocent moment of vulnerability that led to vast speculation. Was Nina *dating* Eddie? Did she know something that the rest of the world did not?

Eddie couldn't leave his house. The studio had a team of bodyguards push through the swarm of media that had set up camp outside his building and whisk him away. They housed him in luxurious accommodation and brought him everything he wanted. He learned that the other remaining actors from the show – Deacon and Francois – had also been moved for their safety.

Each scene they shot was pivotal. Not only did these sequences determine their survival within the show but they were also being edited together to form the final film. This week was the sex scene with Nina Place. The men had been given creative freedom to choreograph the scene as part of the challenge, ensuring that each scene was completely different.

The scenes aired one by one within the live show.

Deacon and Nina's scene involved a steamy make out session in the doorway of her character's apartment. Deacon then – mid kiss – pushed his way inside the room and slammed the door behind him. They moved to the couch and made love.

Francois's scene with Nina was tamer. He had Nina lead him to the bedroom where they acted out some kind of soft-core pornography without ever removing any clothes. At the end of the scene the camera had tastefully panned across to the nightstand to preserve her character's modesty.

Eddie knew there was extra pressure on this scene. He knew people were watching to see whether he and Nina had chemistry. His scene was twice as long as the other two combined. Audiences watched in awe as Eddie threw Nina around the apartment in the throes of passion. They had sex in the kitchen, on the floor and against the wall.

Eddie and Nina agreed that the intensity of the moment required complete nudity. When Eddie showed his rear on screen the audience cheered. They held their breath as the actors pretended to climax together on the floor.

'Amazing!' called the host when the scene faded to black. 'Wow!'

The audience gave him a standing ovation and Eddie found himself with tears in his eyes. He'd never felt so happy and fulfilled before.

The problem was what happened next.

When it came time to vote the general consensus was that either Deacon or Francois would be going home. The campaign to 'Save Deacon' and the rival campaign to 'Save Francois' generated so many votes that in a twist of fate people forgot to vote for Eddie. Everyone assumed that everyone *else* was voting for him. He was eliminated and everyone – including Eddie - was shocked.

But they didn't stay shocked for very long.

The nature of the show meant that Eddie was forgotten in the wake of the show's epic finale. Deacon or Francois would make history and be crowned the winner of *The Leading Man*.

The Producer's wanted to keep making money and so they had another amazing idea. That summer they released both versions of *Explosive Cargo* in theatres. One that starred Deacon Montgomery and one that starred Francois Vutton.

Patrons were invited to watch each film and then cast their ballot for the winning actor.

Deacon won in a landslide.

Eddie tried to be happy in his life. He called Missy and despite the odds the two started dating again.

Eddie continued to act for a while but never achieved any awards or notoriety beyond *The Leading Man*. The show remained popular for years to come. Each time an actor went for an audition anywhere in the world they wondered, in the back of their mind, whether they might find themselves on the next series of *The Leading Man*.

TO WHOM IT MAY CONCERN

If you are reading this then my trip through time has not been in vain. If you are a traveller like me you will no doubt have forgotten your voyage to the present and regrettably, soon I will join you in blissful ignorance. Before it slips away from me I intend to recount to the best of my memory our mission. I tried to bring back hard drives and holograms to better illuminate everything but unfortunately the act of time travel appears to wipe clean all of these devices. The human brain is no different. My knowledge of the future will only last as long as my willpower allows me to retain it. I can already feel a subtle unconscious force clouding my mind.

I should begin.

My name is Max Kibou and I am time traveller number thirty-one. It is my hope that this will reach another time traveller and jog their memory. Maybe I'm writing this to jog my own memory after it fades. I have no idea if this is even possible, as I have never heard from anyone that has been sent back before. We all seem to forget. As far as we can ascertain in the future these trips have had no impact on our future. Yet.

The future I am from is a shadow of the world you know. A series of events have created utter chaos leaving the Earth scorched and in a constant state of civil war.

The act that started this chain of events occurred in 2026. By arming you with all of the information I remember YOU can help save the world. The 'event' was dubbed 'Project Ascension' by the media. A single terrorist attack occurred on May 6th of that year.

We are on the verge of identifying all of the responsible parties in the year 2084 where I am from. Having developed a time travel device we have been systematically sending back agents to alter the events that lead to this attack. If you are reading this and you are one of the terrorists involved I implore you to stop and consider the consequences.

Our tactics have been hard to measure because any changes that occur through our actions have altered our timeline. Perhaps we have had more success than I know. Our theory is that we have made multiple changes so far but we are not exactly sure how effective our moves have been. All of this obviously depends on whether we are in charge of our fate and can change these events at all!

There is also the theory that Project Ascension *must* occur in order for us to create the time travel device in 2084 or there will be a paradox. You wouldn't be reading this if I never wrote it, and I would never have written it if I hadn't travelled back in time to do so.

This may be hard to believe but I promise you this is a horrendous future that is most comparable to hell on Earth.

You should do all you can to stop this outcome.

Project Ascension – or 'the event' - took place in Canberra, Australia. The majority of the Australian Government was meeting in Parliament House to discuss the country's future. The population had just voted to become a Republic, and this would be the first of many Parliamentary meetings to establish a group of interim leaders while Australia voted for its very first President. While the vast majority of Australians wanted to sever ties with the now corrupt British Monarchy there was a selection of rebellious parties that did not want change. One of these factions was responsible for what happened next. A concentrated explosion levelled most of Parliament House killing all elected members in attendance.

Prime Minister Johnson was among those killed. This event stopped the world.

With no central leadership Australia devolved into states and territories. It was not long before the people revolted and the military were dispatched.

I must summarise because time is of the essence.

Everything became regulated by the military and food and water resources were scarce at the best of times. In the years after Project Ascension occurred bombings were a nightly event. The death toll promoted more and more ordinary Australians to join the military.

In a most spiteful turn of events Britain ignored Australia entirely. They had been cast aside and took the opportunity to make an example of the defectors. The dethroning of the Monarchy was intended to be a victory for independence and the new Australia. Since then no country has dared to repeat this offence. American troops came and went and ideas for peace were tried unsuccessfully. Some countries used the Australian situation as an excuse to bomb and invade other countries. Alliances were tested.

Within Australia border patrols sprung up and the citizens became unable to move freely from state to state. Over the course of many years through strategic bombing the population dropped.

Schooling was replaced with training.

Education was replaced with participation.

Places of artistic endeavour became the target of attacks and soon there became a kind of social stigma around creative pursuits.

There was still rioting in the streets but now there was also a black market for guns and bombs that fuelled the fires of war.

I was born in 2052. My friends and I used to get our kicks sneaking as close as we could to the frontline and watching the men and women protecting us from invasion.

We stopped going out after dark when a group known as OTIC started kidnapping and recruiting children for war.

There was a rumour that the military of my future were in cahoots across the country. A group of New South Wales soldiers were given the assignment of digging a secret tunnel into Victoria in order to infiltrate enemy camps. Most of their forces were captured and those that escaped swore that they saw the same commanding officers across the border. Their voices were conveniently silenced during an attack, and no one from that tunnelling mission survived to confirm the details. If they were right - and there are those that believed them in my future - then military forces are fuelling the war and keeping themselves in charge of the country. If it was a lie then it's a crazy thing to just make up.

As I write this now I am in a quiet room with a single window above a flower shop. Your skyline is like nothing I have seen in my life. Where I'm from the time travel device is situated in this same shop geographically. Of course it isn't a flower shop anymore.

Time travel feels like a lot of wind and energy floating around you and then suddenly you're displaced. It makes you disorientated for a moment and then you start to adjust. Although I suppose not everyone adjusted so well.

For security reasons I will not disclose my exact location. To the best of my knowledge whenever we have sent someone back they have landed here, metres from where the device sat in my future. The device does not come back so it is very much a one-way trip.

I appeared about twelve hours ago and was alone for a short time before Dana saw me. She is a beautiful redheaded woman who I have learned owns and runs this shop herself.

She has refused to let me write her last name here and I am more than happy to omit it in exchange for her help. She mistook me for a customer and it has taken me many hours to convince her of the truth. It is far-fetched and I'm not sure I would have believed it myself, if the situation were reversed.

While Dana's shop is a sensory overload the most noticeable scent is her vanilla deodorant. She reminds me of a photograph from an old magazine. Dana assures me she is not a model and has never been photographed. In the future soldiers carry small address books filled with pictures. Most of them are pornographic in nature but many come from old pamphlets and magazines. It might be the only personal art besides tattoos that exists in my time. Haircuts are strictly short and facial hair is usually long as the soldiers shave only when it is convenient. If bombs are dropping nearby men rarely feel safe enough to grab a razor.

I am pleased to be so lucid. It is also an amazing sensation to interact with a past I have heard so much about. It might be akin to sending you back to a time before pollution and having you smell how clean the air can be.

As I mentioned in an attempt to prove my story I brought back various data devices in my jacket but all are blank. We have talked at length and Dana is letting me write the document you are now reading on her laptop. I have never used a laptop in such amazing condition. She seems to be coming around to the facts, and I'm hopeful that she will post this online for me when I can no longer remember to do so. There were some records available to us online about our time travel experiments. There had been police reports about men and women who couldn't remember who they were; all discovered in this area.

Some conspiracy theorists pointed to alien abduction but no one put together a time travel angle.

I guess you all assume from films that memory is not an issue for those that travel through time. We were able to collect some information but there were no images to confirm these reports referred to the previous thirty agents.

In my time we still use Twitter. It was quite a novelty to find out how new it is to you! Our military use it for coordinates, communication and code as there is still roaming Wi-Fi that can be accessed across the nation. People do not stay online for long in the future because hacking is so common. The Internet has become a luxury and although computers are everywhere they are largely communal.

I was recruited around the age of fifteen with a kind of athletic scholarship. I was always the fastest teenager of my friends and the skill of moving quickly translates in the field. My father told me that he had always been fast too. If we still participated in the Olympics he thought he would have qualified with ease.

My mother died when I was young. Her name was Bethany Underwood and she was an administration officer at a small outpost in southern New South Wales. It was relatively close to the border and there had been a kind of 'push and pull' with the Victorian troops stationed nearby. The frontline is the first line of defence and it can be dangerous. A group of trucks approached the outpost where my mother was stationed and sprayed the building with bullets. The attack had been planned at a time between supply drops and the outpost was low on ammunition. The Victorians - knowing this - forced them to deplete their remaining ammo until they were ill equipped to defend themselves. It is unfortunate due to the isolating nature of war that medical supplies have become luxuries. When you are wounded on the frontline it is considered courteous to commit suicide.

This will prevent your probable capture, torture and eventual death. Bethany was able to send a single Tweet before she and the seven others at the outpost took their own lives.

'Outpost has fallen. Standard exit. Tell Max I love him #MTFCBC'

I've read that Tweet on her feed hundreds of times over the years since. I have felt the weight of each word. 'Standard exit' has become a normal way of announcing your suicide. The *standard* way to die in my time is to shoot yourself between the eyes. It was months before I knew what #MTFCBC meant. It was added to several Tweets throughout her military service and often directed to my father Mark. Because I was sent away for training I spent my time trying to decipher what it meant. Eventually I was given the answer from my father.

Mark the future can be changed.

My mother believed this was the only way to save our world. Time travel.

It had been a hot topic throughout my parent's courtship and the hashtag had been a kind of personal joke between them. Maybe in the moment of her death she smiled and knew that this was only one possible future. Time travel had not been perfected – and only thirty-one of us know for sure that it works. We sent back multiple communication attempts but failed to get a response.

I've just been prodded by Dana. I must have dozed off for only a moment as I still feel the same. I still remember.

I was selected for a series of aptitude tests designed to find suitable candidates to send back. The testing related to data retention and mental strength. As you can tell my recall is strong and I remember things easily enough even after my voyage through time. It's a strange sensation. I can feel myself *wanting* to be in the present. I think there must be a kind of reset happening where the information I have relates to only one *possible* future. As I have now made it back to your time I hope my future has changed. If it has, then maybe that's why I am forgetting it, because it has not and will not occur.

Time travel was perfected by a man named Dr Trax Benson. He claimed that a person could theoretically travel backwards and forwards through time and remember everything. It was a dream of his to time travel himself one day. He spoke of meeting his wife again in 2015 and watching his youthful days of falling in love play out. Dr Benson said that the moment he saw his future wife at University was one of his happiest memories. He was a man of science and when pollution ravaged our oceans and drinking water he was charged with creating an alternative. Imagine a powder that you pour into a container and subsequently urinate onto. With the human race using up the Earth's natural resources this became an alternative to drinking water. It is the only available drink to many military components on the frontline. Drinking your own urine may sound ridiculous to you as you live in a world of excess and availability. I should tell you that the powder contains many artificial flavours and usually contains only a trace of urine aftertaste. My favourite flavour is cranberry.

I have been able to sample many of your packaged foods as there is a vending machine outside the flower shop and Dana has kindly purchased them for me. The sugar content is high and I'm not used to it. I am coupling my intake with coffee and sandwiches to avoid crashing. As you may have guessed I'm trying coffee for the first time today. It's an unusual taste but the novelty was one I could not pass up. In my time you could go your entire life without meeting someone that had tasted coffee.

I understand that many of the previous thirty time travellers were dead on arrival. I guess Dr Benson was still working on his device and the settings resulted in many unexpected side effects. I'm thankful I discovered the program when I did and that I'm here and alive to tell the tale.

I had never considered the possibility that I would time travel until two months ago, or depending how you think about it sixty-nine years from now. Following the testing process two of us were selected as potential time travellers. My offsicer Liam had excelled in memory tests and was well built. Liam had tattoos from his neck down to his toes. We spent about a month living in an underground bunker while we trained and got to know each other pretty well. Liam had grown up without a father and seemed to need a strong male influence in his life. The call to arms was a natural one and he seemed relaxed and ready to time travel. One morning I woke up and Liam was gone. Soon after I was asked to prepare myself as I had been chosen. When I was taken and briefed on my mission I couldn't help but wonder why I was going first. Liam was stronger and I had assumed he would excel. There must have been some deficiency I wasn't privy to.

I was asked what date I would like to come back to and I selected today because it is my father's birthday. May 17th 2015. The words of Dr Benson came back to me as I climbed into the device. I thought that if I could choose a moment in the past that I would come back to a time before the war and see my parents. My mother will be born some months from now but I cannot imagine my mind lasting that long. I felt some cosmic symmetry to arriving on the day my father would join the human race.

I love my father.

My name is Dana and I promised Max that I would upload this for him. I don't know whether anything he told me was true. He seemed so sure with each sentence that I must say there were moments when I believed it all. Max was tall and held himself with military posture. When he spoke he curled the edges of his mouth into a smile, which he held between thoughts. I feel I should complete this story for him just in case. If he's telling the truth then the details I leave here may be of some use to you in the future.

We stopped typing and Max convinced me to drive him ten kilometres to see his father. When he first suggested this I had the sudden notion that I would be leaving him there and this would become a strange story I told at parties.

When we got into my car he changed the radio to a frequency they use in the future but all he could hear was static. On the drive he spoke of a band of terrorists from his time and step by step how they executed a plan to decapitate the Statue of Liberty. It was a fantastical story that he used to illustrate how the many cultural landmarks we take for granted in our time have been destroyed in his.

Max spent most of the drive staring out the window. He was squinting at the sun and saying how the sky was different. I reassured him that I believed him and that things would change but he didn't seem to believe me. He said 'everything is temporary' and that we are all in 'a constant state of decay.' He asked me what I wanted from this life and I told him I just wanted to be happy. He asked me what I needed to make myself happy and I told him I didn't know.

'Well, you had better figure it out fast. The world is ending,' was his reply.

We listened to music on the drive as I tried to process it all. When we arrived at his father's house at dusk there was a dark red van parked in the driveway with a couple embracing nearby. This couple then retrieved a baby capsule from inside the van and the sound of my engine was replaced by the cries of this child. I assume the child was Max's father Mark. When I looked over to Max for a reaction he seemed catatonic He had great big beads of sweat pouring down his face and past his nose as he stared out of the windscreen. He was physically changed as if a sudden fever had come on out of nowhere.

Max never spoke to me again.

He has been placed in a care facility and I have visited him several times but he has remained silent. I think the sight of his father as a child triggered something in him. Maybe it was another of Max's paradoxes.

I have a bad feeling everything is happening as it always did.

Maybe I'm becoming paranoid but I think that this story will find its way to Mark and he will recognise something in it. When he grows up he will meet a woman named Bethany Underwood and know instinctively they will be together. Maybe he shows her this story. Maybe that's why they will make time travel a personal joke between them.

The terrorist act will happen as scheduled and Mark will know the story is true.

Just knowing that *this* might be the inspiration for the terrorist act itself has given me many sleepless nights.

Imagine if Mark and Bethany have a child and they name him Max and one day he comes back in time and meets me. Am I helping create the future he was trying to change? Is this having any effect on the time stream at all?

To my reader - I don't know who you are, or *when* you are but I hope you can help. In my mind #MTFCBC now stands for 'Max the future can be changed.' Maybe it always did.

Six days after I met Max on May 23rd 2015 I found a dead person in my flower shop. It was the body of a shirtless man whose throat had been slashed and the blood drained from his body.

I don't know whether this man was sent back during your time travel tests but I thought it was important to tell you that all his tattoos were intact. If you have a message from the future you should tattoo it onto the next person you send back. If you do, I will get your message and I will know Max was telling the truth. I have left my car radio on that AM frequency but I'm only hearing static.

DON'T WANT TO MISS A THING

I can't believe that we're finally here! Lucy looks so hot tonight. I'm so glad she looks like her profile picture. I wish the mall wasn't so busy. Coming to the mall for a first date might have been a bad idea. Oh well. At least there are lots of places we can eat.

'So what do you feel like eating Lucy?'

'Um…whatever.'

She's got such great legs. They look so good in that short skirt. I hope she lets me put my hand on her leg in the cinema.

'Let's get Chinese food. Cool?'

'Yeah cool.'

Alright let's see… what should I get? I'll probably have to pay for hers too. I don't really feel like rice… Just meat maybe? What would THAT be like? Meat with no rice.

'Hey have you ever had meat with no rice?'

'No.'

'Me neither. I think I'm going to get it.'

'Ew. Why?'

'I like meat. I don't really feel like rice.'

'But you need the rice to be like…a *base*… don't you?'

'I don't know. I think it'll be fine.'

She just smiled at me. This is going great! Time to get to know her a bit while we eat.

'So how many brothers and sisters do you have?'

'One brother and one sister.'

'Are you the middle child?'

'The youngest.'

'That's cool.'

'Do you have a big family?'

'Nah…just me and my Dad.'

She's not eating much. Maybe she wants popcorn later. I hate how expensive movie food is. Maybe I should suggest we go to the supermarket beforehand and get some snacks. That might make me look cheap. What should I suggest then? We still have some time before the movie.

'So do you want to do a little shopping after we eat? The movie doesn't start for about an hour.'

'Yeah I guess so.'

…

Don't overthink it! It's going well. No it's going GREAT! Yeah…it's the best. You're the man Vin. Tell her your story about meeting Hugh Jackman. She'll be impressed. Everyone likes Hugh Jackman.

'Did I ever tell you I once met Hugh Jackman?'

'You did?'

'Yeah.'

'That's cool.'

'Have you ever met anyone famous?'

'Um…not really. I went and waved at Kate Middleton when she was in town with William.'

'Kate... who?'

'Never mind.'

...

Alright...shopping. This will be fun. Maybe she'll do something sexy like buy some lingerie. Then she could try it on for me later. I hope we hook up tonight. It's been a while for me. What kind of stuff was she into in her profile again? I can't remember.

'That's nice.'

'What is?'

'That top. That would look g- '

...

Uhhh...

...

'Are you alright?'

'Fine.'

Oooh... that meat isn't sitting well. I've got to put some distance between us so I can fart. Be smooth Vin...

'Are you sure you're alright?'

'I'm *so* fine. Hey, let's go down this escalator and see what they have downstairs.'

'Okay.'

Careful now...Ahhhhhh! There it goes. And she's none the wiser. It's a good thing that we're heading down the escalator rather than up. All that meat really WAS a bad idea. Oh well. I've gotten away with it. A few minutes more of looking at clothes and I'll suggest we head up to see the movie. I can't wait to see this freaking movie! It's going to be so good. I wonder if Lucy will like it.

'Do you think we should go?'

'Ok sure. If you're done shopping?'

'I'm fine. Let's go.'

…

Should I hold her hand? Maybe I should wait until we're actually in our seats. Alright…got the tickets. Let's see if she's hungry.

'Did you want popcorn?'

'No…I'm alright. Unless you do?'

'Nah…I'm still full.'

'From the meat?'

'Yeah.'

I should have taken her to this movie next week. It's so busy tonight!

'Where do you want to sit?'

'Anywhere is fine.'

Hmmm… my stomach is doing something weird. Do I have time to go to the bathroom before the movie? Probably not. I'll be fine.

'Let's sit on the aisle.'

So I can get up if I need to. It's good to have an exit strategy.

'This is fun.'

'Yeah.'

Alright...Whoa! Amazing helicopter scene to open the film. What was the budget on this thing anyway? There have been at least six explosions and the film isn't even halfway through. Why did I eat that meat without rice? It needed a base. I feel like I'm going to shit my pants. Goddamn it!

...

'Psst...Hey Lucy?'

'What is it?'

'Listen...this is going to sound kind of weird but I'm really enjoying the movie.'

'Yeah me too.'

'Right... and I sort of need to go to the bathroom.'

'So go...'

'But I don't want to miss anything.'

'Do you want me to tell you what happens when you get back?'

'No I hate that. Then we'll both miss stuff while you're telling me...'

'I don't mind Vin...'

'Nah...I've got a better idea. I'll call you now and you hold up the phone so I can listen until I get back.'

'Really?'

'Is that okay?'

'Um...if you want...'

'Thanks.'

This is perfect. It's working... Was that another explosion? Jesus this film is great.

...

Oh man...I'll never go back to that Chinese place.

...

I'm glad I'm the only one in here...ugh that stinks...

...

This is disgusting.

...

Gross...

...

Goddamn... I feel like a new man.

...

Much better.

...

I can't believe he took me to the mall. This guy is such a scrub. What kind of a name is Vin anyway? Is it short for Vinnie or Vincent? I miss Zach. I can't believe he's going out with that whore Tiffany. I told him I wouldn't wait around for him. He thinks he can fuck her and then come back to me? Hell no. I won't stand for it.

'So what do you feel like eating Lucy?'

'Um...whatever.'

Food court food and a movie... Are we twelve? I don't even care anymore. Zach's brother works at the movies and I need to be seen. He will definitely tell Zach that he saw me tonight and then he'll know I'm not alone at home crying over him.

'Let's get Chinese food. Cool?'

'Yeah cool.'

Vin had better be paying for this Chinese food. Maybe I'll just get an appetiser.

'Hey have you ever had meat with no rice?'

'No.'

'Me neither. I think I'm going to get it.'

'Ew. Why?'

'I like meat. I don't really feel like rice.'

'But you need the rice to be like…a base… don't you?'

'I don't know. I think it'll be fine.'

God…smile politely Lucy. It's just for the night. This guy seems like an idiot. Is eating meat with no rice supposed to impress me? I don't really eat a lot of meat. And now he's staring at me…

'So how many brothers and sisters do you have?'

'One brother and one sister.'

'Are you the middle child?'

'The youngest.'

'That's cool.'

I guess I'd better ask him the same question back. I don't want to come off as rude…

'Do you have a big family?'

'Nah…just me and my Dad.'

That's it. This is now officially awkward. I miss Zach. He was so good at opening me up. I always wanted to talk to him all night. We never had any awkward pauses.

'So do you want to do a little shopping after we eat? The movie doesn't start for about an hour.'

'Yeah I guess so.'

…

I've got to try not to walk right next to him. I don't want him to get the wrong idea here. This date is a one-time thing…

'Did I ever tell you I once met Hugh Jackman?'

'You did?'

'Yeah.'

'That's cool.'

'Have you ever met anyone famous?'

'Um…not really. I went and waved at Kate Middleton when she was in town with William.'

'Kate… who?'

'Never mind.'

…

He doesn't even know who Kate Middleton is. We are so incompatible! I'll just look at clothes. What is this gross colour?

I would never wear this.

'That's nice.'

'What is?'

'That top. That would look g- '

…

What the fuck is wrong with this guy? He looks like he's going to throw up!

'Are you alright?'

'Fine.'

'Are you sure you're alright?'

'I'm *so* fine. Hey, let's go down this escalator and see what they have downstairs.'

'Okay.'

I should check Instagram and see if Zach liked my picture. I only posted it a couple of hours ago. Will he have seen it? I'll bet he still thinks about me. Going on this date with Vin was a mistake. Vincenzo? Maybe he's Italian? We should just go to the cinema so we can stop talking.

'Do you think we should go?'

'Ok sure. If you're done shopping?'

'I'm fine. Let's go.'

…

No comments from Zach. That's alright… his brother just saw me. Yep…it's me. Don't I look good? Tell Zach what he's missing out on! This mini skirt was a good idea.

'Did you want popcorn?'

Yes…NO! I shouldn't.

'No…I'm alright. Unless you do?'

'Nah…I'm still full.'

'From the meat?'

'Yeah.'

Even though I'd rather be here with Zach I do kind of want to watch this movie. It looked good from the previews. Maybe Zach will be here tonight. He wanted to see it too. He's probably brought that whore though. Is that him? No… It's too dark to see…

'Where do you want to sit?'

'Anywhere is fine.'

'Let's sit on the aisle.'

I don't see him. That's probably for the best. I mean I want him to get jealous but if he actually saw Vin he might not care. It's better that his brother tells him. Then he'll build it up in his mind. He'll call…I know he will. Why are we sitting on the aisle? I hate being on an angle like this.

'This is fun.'

'Yeah.'

I'll get someone else to pick me up after this. I don't want Vin to know where I live. Whoa… that guy on screen is pretty buff. Now I wish I had popcorn.

…

'Psst…Hey Lucy?'

'What is it?'

'Listen…this is going to sound kind of weird but I'm really enjoying the movie.'

'Yeah me too.'

'Right… and I sort of need to go to the bathroom.'

'So go…'

'But I don't want to miss anything.'

'Do you want me to tell you what happens when you get back?'

'No I hate that. Then we'll both miss stuff while you're telling me…'

I'm missing stuff right now you wanker…

'I don't mind Vin…'

'Nah…I've got a better idea. I'll call you now and you hold up the phone so I can listen until I get back.'

'Really?'

'Is that okay?'

Whatever it takes to get rid of you.

'Um…if you want…'

'Thanks.'

…

I guess I'll just hold this phone then. I feel like an idiot. I figured Vin was nice but he's barely asked me anything. Maybe this was a ploy? He wanted to get my number! Of course! That's actually pretty smart. This movie is really good too. I get it. I kind of need to pee but I'll wait. It must be almost over. I'll pee afterwards. Hey my phone just buzzed.

It's Zach!

Should I answer it? Oh shit! SHIT. I put Vin on SPEAKERPHONE!!!

FUCK!

What is THAT noise?

FUCK...I just dropped my phone.

...

FUCK.

...

WHERE THE FUCK IS IT?

Is he taking a...

SHIT.

He IS!

OH FUCK. THAT IS DISGUSTING.

JESUS FUCKING CHRIST. VIN!

This is SO EMBARRASING!

Where is that PHONE?

...

Hang up...

...

Oh my GOD this whole cinema is laughing. They just heard Vin taking a shit.

Oh FUCK.

...

This is so mortifying.

Well I have to leave.

FORTUNE TELLER

When he was twelve years young Nathan Beck was told by a fortune teller at a carnival that he would die at the age of thirty-three. It was such a strange and specific prediction that he wrote it down in the back of his diary. He then kept that diary and reminded himself of that day whenever his birthday came around. If it was true, Nathan thought, he'd be safe and happy *until* the age of thirty-three. This could be a free pass to attempt any dangerous stunts and reckless activities knowing that he couldn't – and *wouldn't* - die. He then considered that he might end up in a coma or some kind of vegetative state and end up dying at the age of thirty-three anyway. Nathan was at a loss at what should he do with this amazing knowledge.

The fortune teller's words made him extremely careful. Nathan suddenly understood the value of his life, now that it had a theoretical conclusion. He travelled back to that same carnival year after year but he could never find that fortune teller again. He had his fortune re-told over the years but each time he found himself sceptical of any new information. In Nathan's mind, that first fortune teller was right and he couldn't be convinced of anything else. He grew up and tried to forget his impending death but it was always there in the back of his mind.

At the age of nineteen he fell in love with a beautiful woman named Penelope. They took an overseas holiday together to Scotland where they stayed with her Grandparents to save money. One night at the dinner table Nathan decided to confide in the group and he told them about the fortune teller.

'He told me that I would die at the age of thirty-three,' he said as he finished telling the tale. 'I've never forgotten it.'

'Surely you don't believe that?' said Penelope's Grandfather in a booming voice.

'I can't explain it but somehow I know it's true.'

'Don't you think that life plays out the way it plays out? Things aren't so *determined* like that,' stated Penelope.

'I know what you mean and I assure you I *want* you to be right. I have just always felt like he spoke the truth.'

'How could he know the future?' asked Penelope's Grandmother.

'There's no way he could I suppose. But it felt real.'

'I guess the only way to know with any certainty is to wait until you're thirty-four!' said Penelope as she planted a kiss on Nathan's cheek.

He smiled and life carried on. Penelope and Nathan broke up when, at the age of twenty-two, another woman – named Mary - caught his eye.

'How *could* you?' Penelope seethed when she found out the truth about Nathan and Mary.

'It just happened,' he said. 'I don't know what to say.'

Penelope's now red hair accentuated the fire in her eyes and she spewed expletives at Nathan. She concluded by telling him that she hoped the fortune teller was right and that he dropped dead.

Nathan and Mary's relationship was short lived. She thought the idea of marriage was antiquated and didn't ever see herself as a mother. The whole thing fizzled out due to a lack of momentum. Neither party felt like there was anywhere to go or anything to achieve between them. It ended amicably.

Nathan's father died when he was twenty-six. It led to a period of reflection and obsession. He became obsessed with his health and obsessed with his legacy. If the fortune teller was right and Nathan had only seven years left to live then he would make sure they were the best and most fruitful years of his life.

Nathan became the best possible version of himself. He exercised every morning as the sun came up; he ate organically and was nice to everyone he met. He made friends easily and attended all manner of social events. He didn't drink or smoke or take recreational drugs. He worked as a delivery driver but made a conscious effort to donate to charity and volunteer his time whenever he could.

One day when he was working as a volunteer at a local charity shop he met Georgia. She had a glass half full approach to life that Nathan loved. She believed in people and wanted to make the world a better place. Their shared optimism became the foundation of their relationship and, due to a combination of carelessness and passion the couple found themselves pregnant.

'That's amazing news!' Nathan said and hugged her.

Georgia wasn't so sure. Nathan had told her about the fortune teller and he'd been very convincing about his fate.

'I don't want to lose you Nathan. If we raise this baby then I want to do it together.'

'I *want* you to have this baby. I've never wanted anything more!'

Nathan was scared but he knew that if they aborted the baby he wouldn't have had any impact on the world. He selfishly wanted to become a father so that his life wouldn't have been in vain. Somehow Nathan hid all of his insecurities and maintained a façade of confidence for long enough to dispel Georgia's concerns.

Their daughter Grace was born three days after Nathan's twenty-eighth birthday. She was premature and although she seemed too small to survive, somehow she did. As she grew up Nathan found he loved being a father and wondered if Georgia would consider expanding their family.

Their son Isaac was also premature but sadly he did not survive. Georgia was done after that. She refused to entertain the idea of going through such a terrible loss again – especially when she might lose Nathan in just a few short years. They set aside their differences and took a beachside holiday for Nathan's thirtieth birthday.

As Grace grew up she became a ball of curiosity. Nathan made the mistake of watching the news with her one day. She began questioning the world and why bad things happened.

'What happened on the news?'

'There was a fire.'

'Why did that car crash?'

'They were driving too fast.'

The news was always grim but it wasn't until her goldfish died that the concept of death was introduced to Grace in a very real way.

'But I don't want to die!'

'You won't have to die for a very long time. You'll grow up and become an old lady.'

'I don't want to be an *old lady*!' she protested.

At the age of four she was too young to understand. Her fifth birthday would almost coincide with Nathan's thirty-third. His final year of life was imminent. Georgia didn't know what to do for the occasion.

'We've dreaded this day for so long that I didn't know how to plan for it. I didn't know how you would feel. Is there anything you want to do?'

'It's alright,' he said. 'I've accepted it. Whatever happens now is the way it has to be. I love you and I love Grace and I love our life. I don't want it to end but I'm so glad it has been as happy and fulfilled as this.'

The two shared a passionate kiss and Nathan had a crazy idea.

'Marry me,' he said quickly.

'What?'

'That's what I want for my birthday. Marry me.'

Georgia smiled and wiped a small tear that was gliding down her cheek.

'Alright.'

After Grace's fifth birthday they were married. Nathan spent his thirty-third year on Earth writing letters to his wife and daughter that they would read after his death. He became present for the first time in his life. He enjoyed every moment and felt every emotion he was capable of. Every night when he went to sleep he wondered if it would be his last. He tried to be positive but the idea of death was terrifying. He didn't want to miss out on seeing his daughter grow up. He didn't want to leave Georgia alone. Long ago Nathan had taken out a hefty life insurance policy that he had dutifully paid in the years since. If he died at least his family would be taken care of financially. This was the only advantage to knowing the future.

As the year wore on they celebrated every day as if it were Nathan's last. During their final Christmas as a family Nathan couldn't explain to Grace why Georgia was crying so much.

He just hugged them both and tried to smile despite the weight of expectation.

As his thirty-fourth birthday approached Nathan imagined a guillotine hovering overhead – waiting to drop. He became sad and inconsolable. He had taken time off from work and spent most days in a hammock in the backyard. A week before his birthday he was filled with a mix of hope and fear.

This was it.

Either the fortune teller was psychic and he was about to die or... *or what?*

His entire life had been a lie? He'd made choices based off something that had happened when he was twelve. He didn't think they were *bad* choices necessarily... just cautious ones. He was happy enough. Nathan just didn't want it to end.

And it didn't.

At least it didn't end by his thirty-fourth birthday as predicted. The fortune teller was actually a disgruntled employee who was fired shortly after giving that prediction to Nathan. He was tired of pretending to know the future and particularly bitter about his wife leaving him for a circus strong man. He had been drinking excessively and spouting rubbish to anyone that asked for their fortune. Nathan was particularly gullible at the time and the information resonated with him more than it should have.

His single bad day ruined the first half of Nathan's life.

AFTER THE MOVIE

I hit the *Start* button.

The Projector comes to life with a mechanical roar. I inspect the 35mm film as it flows easily through the cogs and over the rollers. The fluorescent light hits the rundown leader that has been handled by so many projectionists over the years. I check and double check each turn the film will make during playout. I probably have a mild case of OCD and for a projectionist that might not be the worst thing. If a single roller is missed or the film is sitting incorrectly then it will be damaged. The print will be scratched beyond repair. Everything has to be set up exactly right *every* time.

The house lights are on and I can see the theatre is starting to fill up. People don't go to the movies like they used to. This dying art will soon be replaced with digital files and digital projectionists. Everything will be automated. Each time you see a film it will be perfect and exactly as the Director intended. This means that projectionists like me won't be needed and the only jobs for us will be at Archives.

I suppose true fans of celluloid like Quentin Tarantino and those who have their own cinemas will still employ people like me. Or maybe they will just learn to thread a projector themselves. Maybe QT will make a film about a projectionist one day. There was a projectionist in *Inglourious Basterds* so I guess he already has. The coolest projectionist committed to celluloid would have to be Tyler Durden (from David Fincher's *Fight Club*) but he's really more into mayhem than correct cinematic presentation. I'm sure we've all thought about splicing porn into a print like he did. The projectionist is the variable when you go to the movies.

If I do my job right then no one should give me a second thought. I guess it's kind of thankless. Doing it right is what is expected.

The bare minimum if you will. A quote from Martin Scorsese hangs on the wall above the projector.

The Projectionist makes the final cut.

That gives me an idea for a film about a killer projectionist! When you do nothing but watch movies all night you tend to come up with ideas for them on a regular basis. The projectionist could stalk his victims from above and then get them from behind as they sit in the back rows. It would be dark so no one would catch on until after the movie ends and they discover the body. *Watch at your own risk.* Now there's a tagline. I'll make a quick note on the back of my program before I forget.

I can run a dozen sessions a night on my own. Patrons will waltz in and see their film and so rarely even glance to the back of the cinema. Far too often I look down to find people dry humping or worse. Each time I tell someone at a party what I do they make it seem trivial. The common misconception is that the projector can be paused or rewound if you're running late. People think projectionists just push a button and everything happens. In the words of Rusty Ryan - portrayed by Brad Pitt - from Steven Soderbergh's *Ocean's Eleven*: *'Slightly more complicated than that.'*

Tonight I'm doing a favour for a friend and working his shift at the University. It's a complicated set up for any projectionist for two reasons:

1 – Normally the films are delivered in numbered reels and taped together as one giant print. The print is then fed through the projector and plays as one big piece. To use a visual example imagine a cassette tape - if you're old enough to remember them.

The tape is all on one side and as it plays through it ends up on the other. In the case of the University projectors I would like to stress: They are old. They don't have the space or the right equipment to combine all the reels. So tonight I'll be playing the film using two projectors and changing reels manually. When the first spool is about to end I'll start the second one and seamlessly flip between them. This means I'll be busy for the whole night. If I'm not paying attention I'm sure to make a mistake. If I'm not ready with the next piece then I'll ruin the experience.

2 - The University is a 'cinema' in the sense that it was a lecture theatre first and a cinema second. This means that it has massive design flaws. The patrons pass the Projection room on their way into the cinema. Many patrons pop their head in to see the projectors, or find out who will be showing the film. The University attracts former students and so this is just the established tradition. Projectionists haven't had this kind of relationship with patrons since the Academy Award winning *Cinema Paradiso*. I imagine there was a time when it first started 40 years ago that everyone knew the projectionist on duty and said hello. I'm a little less social and leave the door closed. This of course only deters those who have not mastered the doorknob! The worst thing is if something does go wrong people come up to stickybeak.

For a long time I had nightmares about projection rooms full of patrons, each criticising my work and getting in my way. Things would break off the projector and then people would be looking at me for answers. You know you are too invested when you bring your work home with you like that.

A door opens to my right. Instinctively I know what this will be about.

'Oh hi,' says an unsure voice.

The man in the doorway looks as though he is the 'before' picture in every exercise infomercial ever made.

'How's it going?' I shoot back.

'Good thanks.'

He is nervous and asks his question as though I have all the answers to the mysteries of the universe.

'I was just wondering what this song is… the one that's playing now?'

This is one of the few perks of working at the University. You can play whatever you like so long as it doesn't have any swearing in it. I use this perk to play obscure film related songs and see if anyone knows what they are from. I like to think people enjoy it and sing along but since the projection booth is almost completely sound proof I have never confirmed this.

I check the CD player and tell him he's listening to 'The Touch' by Stan Bush. He happily leaves the projection room and I see him return to his friends through the porthole. He either knows the song from *Boogie Nights* or the *Transformers* cartoon movie. I feel pretty smug about the exchange. This is my only way of communicating with the crowd and my only chance to make any kind of impression. I want them to like the pre-show entertainment and then wonder who that awesome projectionist was.

My phone buzzes in my pocket. I know its Alana before I check it.

Alana is an art student I have been seeing. What I like about Alana is that I never know what's going to happen with her. She has the body of a model and the face of the girl next door. That might sound like her face doesn't match her body but I think you'll find it's what most guys want. If a woman has the face *and* the body of a model then she's probably a model. And you don't want that drama.

One night I accidently left my leather wrist cuff in her car. I messaged her and asked when I could get it back. She let me know that it was art now. I later learned that she had incorporated the cuff into one of her pieces. Since that happened I have become extremely vigilant about checking the seat as I get out of any car. A friend of mine asked if I had left it in the car so that I would have a way of seeing her again. Sadly I'm just prone to losing things.

I have been trying to close the deal with Alana and I've invited her over after I finish work tonight. The message on my phone is a huge disappointment to my ego.

She's busy.

What's she busy with? Why can't she get busy with me? Since I haven't slept with Alana I consider the possibility that she is horribly disfigured in some unknown way. There really isn't a way to find that out without sleeping together though.

I've got nothing but time alone with my thoughts in the projection room. The nearby speaker makes it possible for me to hear the film but because the projectors are right next to it I have to strain. I think it's a film noir and I'm sure I've missed too much plot to catch up.

I complete the first reel change and start loading up the third spool. Lacing the projector with ease I shut the gate and look at the film.

It's the wrong way around!

If I play this through the film is going to be back to front on the screen. I cut the film with scissors and rush over to my workbench. Spools are either Head or Tail out. I checked each one was Head out before the film started out in this case some lovely projectionist (whoever has played this film last) has joined the tail of this spool to the head incorrectly. I start winding the film as fast as I can by hand. I can see the projector as I wind and the reel growing slowly smaller as it plays through.

I think of the opening sequence of *The Rules of Attraction* playing in reverse.

I'm running out of time. I think of Christopher Nolan's *Memento* – a film that plays in reverse intentionally. I hustle trying to fix the film spool as fast as I can. It is at this horrible moment that Alana rings me.

I can't answer.

My commitment to the quality of this presentation may cost me my night with her. I convince myself that she will call back as I finish rewinding the film. I have mere minutes until this reel is supposed to be on screen. I thread like the wind. I lace with the terrifying image of a cinema full of curious film buffs crowding around me and wondering what I did wrong. I check the gate once more.

Perfect.

I wait until I see the cigarette burn (the cue to start rolling the second projector) in the top-right corner. I hit start. I complete the changeover and wipe beads of sweat from my brow. Nobody in the cinema is aware of what I have just been through. They don't care. There were no witnesses to my struggle. Life goes on without a voicemail from Alana.

Damn.

The rest of the night is much smoother. I find time to text Alana but get no response. We're not officially together yet but the dating has been fun. I think she likes me. She called me and I only texted her. She *must* like me.

I look down on the patrons below. Through the porthole I'm eye level with the screen and using the speaker I listen to the film.

I catch a scene filled with exposition and I'm able to fill in the plot pretty well. This handsome leading man is being cheated on.

What a bozo. It's completely unrealistic and cheesy too. It's hard to believe this guy wouldn't notice it.

It's all over her face. My mind flashes to some of my favourite recent films about infidelity.

Take this Waltz, Swimfan and *Match Point*. For some reason a lot of people think of *Unfaithful* starring Diane Lane. I hated that movie. *High Fidelity* was great too. I guess being cheated on can result in some great art. I wonder how many paintings and songs have been inspired by such betrayal. I have too much time on my hands up here.

Eventually the final reel is loaded and I leave the projection room. The projectors are pretty loud although when they aren't running they have a hypnotic hum. Ben Burtt, the sound designer on *Star Wars*, has been quoted as saying that the sound of the lightsaber was taken from the sound of a film projector idling combined with the feedback of a broken television. I stand at the back of the theatre and wait for the movie to end. I have spoiled so many films this way. I wish I had never watched the end of *Saw* years ago and ruined one of the best twists in modern cinema history. I watch the reactions of the audience. Some have slumped in their seats so much that they have almost disappeared from view. I check my phone: nothing. It's getting late and Alana wont call me back now.

It's annoying that she didn't leave a message. I turn on the house lights just as the credits start. These patrons remind me of Dawson - played by James Van Der Beek - from *Dawson's Creek*. He would always make his friends watch the credits in full - out of respect for all of the people who worked on the film. I always find things like that amusing. The worst is when people applaud after a film. It would be one thing if the film were playing at the Cannes Film Festival or if the Director was present but to just applaud *Shrek* because you liked it seems silly to me.

I could have been with Alana tonight but now I'm wondering whether I've messed it up. It's not a good sign when a woman stops messaging you. I listened to the audiobook of *Men are from Mars and Women are from Venus* last week while I was driving around and it made me paranoid. I figure that if Alana gives me another chance I won't waste it. Maybe I could take her to an outdoor cinema or to a restaurant again. We went to an Indian place for lunch once. It was a first for me and I didn't realise that we would be eating with our hands. I think in a way it was more intimate than it should have been. Our hands didn't touch accidently or anything. It wasn't like *Lady and the Tramp* but it was pretty romantic. I haven't had a girlfriend in ages. It would be nice to be dating someone again, even if it's only for a while.

Before I know it I'm unlocking my car and throwing in my messenger bag. Most of the older crowd loiters around after the movie to chat. It's a surprisingly social group. I have a short drive home ahead of me, and no idea what is about to happen.

I'm cruising along in my aging Ford Cortina towards a T intersection when it happens. Maybe Alana can tell I'm thinking of her. Maybe her ears are burning - or whatever - because she calls me again! I'm keen to answer so I can salvage the evening. Unfortunately there is nowhere to stop here. At the T intersection I slow to turn left where I can pull over more easily. Even though it's late at night there are a few cars around. As I slow and begin turning left I notice a lone cyclist waiting for me. Then, as I'm turning left, he decides to roll out directly in front of my car. I slam on the brakes but I still make contact – barely. It's enough to topple him off his bike. Shit! I hear my phone stop ringing.

If I'm not paying attention I'm sure to make a mistake.

I get out of the car and say something like 'Are you alright?' but because my mind is going a million miles an hour I can't be sure what I actually say. He's probably a student from the campus because he's wearing a backpack and riding a bike at night. He's of Asian appearance and is immediately aggressive. I guess since I just hit him with my car he has the right to be a little ticked off.

'Why did you hit me?' he blurts at me.

'I didn't think you would go,' I stammer.

That was a weak response. I glance at my car and see no sign of damage, which confirms to me that I barely touched him. Although I suppose when you hit someone with your car the person will be worse for wear than the car is. I help my new friend up and find his front tyre has been bent slightly. As I slammed on the brakes I had instinctively turned my steering wheel to avoid hitting him. Looks like all those driving lessons paid off!

I ask him if he's okay as I help him up. He says he is fine but maintains a quiet rage, as he stands upright. I see a group of three girls walking towards the city. They yell across the street to see whether we're okay. I tell them we are and they fade into the night. At this point I realise that my car is stopped in the middle of the road. I take a moment to move it out of the way. For the briefest time the Asian man stares daggers at me because I must look like I'm getting ready to make a run for it.

I have only ever dialled 000 once in my life. When I was about twelve or thirteen years old I stayed home from school with my mum with the intention of 'helping around the house' but my personal mission was to win *X-Men* on the Sega Mega Drive. I managed to spend most of the day living my dream but at around 4.30pm the impending arrival of my father shocked me into action.

If I had stayed home and done nothing all day I would be in trouble. It's funny how as a kid 'trouble' was enough of a motivator.

I jumped up and immediately asked my mum what I could do to help. She put me to work digging holes in the front yard.

This was perfect because then my father would see me working as he arrived home. I started digging and made decent progress on a hole. After about five minutes I found I was hitting some kind of plastic sheet. I kept digging and clinked my shovel straight into a gas pipe. Gas came spewing out rapidly with such force that it hit me in the face. I stumbled backwards partially from the shock but mostly from the potent fumes.

I didn't know what to do.

I kicked a pile of dirt onto the pipe and stomped it down. I remember having to do that a few times before the gas was blocked. 'Police, Fire or Ambulance?' came the voice down the line. It wasn't a police matter as no crime was really committed. Since no one was hurt I said 'fire' as it felt the closest to the truth of the situation. The most vivid memory of the whole mess was my father's face as he drove up the driveway to see the flashing lights of a fire engine parked ahead of him and three firemen towering over his son. I was later informed that if I had somehow created a spark with the shovel that the whole neighbourhood could have been in trouble.

Luckily the only one in trouble was me.

I think about how easy it would be to drive away from the scene of my latest accident. He's disorientated and maybe he wouldn't have the presence of mind to get my plates. Why don't I have revolving fake plates like in *James Bond*? Maybe there would be CCTV cameras though. I know he's okay but I can't leave the scene of an accident. Aren't you supposed to report accidents within 24 hours or something? My first accident. What an exciting time!

The man is sitting on the kerb now and he's taken off his bike helmet. An odd sensation falls over me. His right hand is on his neck. I think back on all the con man films I have seen and wonder if he is going to claim he is more hurt than he first thought.

Does he have some existing injury that I will now be forced to pay for? Was he waiting for me at that crossing? It's clear that I have to tread carefully here.

'Feeling alright?' I ask as I stand over him. It would be weird to sit next to him.

'I don't know why you hit me', he replies.

I should have been home by now.

'Can I take you somewhere?' I offer.

He stares at the sidewalk.

'Can I give you a lift home? Or… to the hospital?'

This gets his attention.

'Can you take me to the hospital then?'

'Sure.'

I pack his bike in the back of my car and he takes the front passenger seat without a word. Before I get back behind the wheel I look back at the scene of the crime. There is a medium sized skid mark where I must have slammed on my brakes. I see the group of girls in the distance laughing as they walk. At least someone is having fun.

The conversation on the way to the hospital is awkward to say the least. I learn his name is Lee and that I was right about him being a student. Lee seems genuinely confused as to why I hit him and keeps asking me about it. I've driven that same road home every night after working at the Uni.

Was it a zebra crossing? Why can't I remember? If it's a zebra crossing I should have given way to Lee and I'm in the wrong. If it's not a zebra crossing then he should have given way to me. I think about the Ben Affleck film *Changing Lanes* where an accident with Samuel L. Jackson's character causes him to miss out on a job interview and ruins his life.

Clearly Lee has nowhere to be because he seems in no rush to get to the hospital. He has stopped holding his neck though and seems able to turn it as he talks to me. Maybe he isn't conning me after all.

What else can I do here? I'm driving him to the hospital *and* making small talk with him. I'm probably the nicest guy that's ever crashed into him too. I feel like I'm floating above the whole surreal scene. I'm definitely going to have to drive him to the Police Station after this. I'm going to miss *Letterman*.

We arrive at the hospital and I park in the 'No Parking' zone straight away. It's less about me being a rebel and more about me not wanting to lug a bike too far. He starts to go in ahead of me and I wheel in his bike. His hand is on the back of his head again.

Original.

The only part of the hospital that is accessible at this time of night is Emergency. I head up to the nurse at the desk.

'Hi, um… this is Lee. I hit him with my car.'

I'm met with a look of shock. I begin to explain that it was at a really slow speed and that I'm bringing him here as a precaution but her eyes look past me to Lee. I turn just in time to see him fall to the ground.

Right...

He looks like he's rolling his eyes back in his head. Is he pretending?

Two nurses come out from behind the desk and examine him.

Suddenly I'm filled with anger about this whole situation.

Lee is really ruining my night with this act. If it is an act...

He's helped onto a mobile hospital bed with wheels. He seems to need little assistance, which makes me really sceptical about his injuries. There was a slight language barrier in the car. I think back on the conversation and decide that he can't have brain damage because he was alert and very quick to respond when we spoke.

The nurses pump me for all the information I know about Lee as we push down a corridor and through two sets of double doors. It feels like I'm in an episode of *Scrubs* or maybe *ER*. It quickly becomes apparent that all I know is that Lee is a student and that he rides a bicycle. I'm not family so I'm sure I won't be sitting at his bedside.

Right on cue a nurse directs me to follow her back the way we came. We take a left instead of a right and suddenly I'm disorientated. She stops in a doorway and gestures for me to go in. I step into the room and she says 'Wait here for me' as she closes the door. It is at this point that I realise there is no handle on my side. She's locked me in!

I didn't see this one coming.

The room is small and a dirty shade of white. I know immediately that there have been a number of unsavoury characters locked in this room before me. It reminds me of every interrogation room I've ever seen on film. I share the room with a table and a security camera that watches me from the ceiling. The missing cliché is the one-way glass. If this were a Police Station they would have taken my shoelaces. My older sister was arrested for shoplifting and while she waited for our dad to pick her up they stuck her in a holding cell like this and took her shoelaces. They told her it was standard procedure. After I heard that I thought about the criminals that must have tried to hang themselves using their shoelaces. I wonder what intense crime they committed to think that death was the only way out. And death by shoelace hanging no less!

I cover every inch of the room in the first thirty seconds. I think back on the nurse telling me to wait here. Do I really have a choice? I'm surprisingly calm considering I'm a prisoner. Maybe not as cool as Wentworth Miller in *Prison Break* but he was far more prepared for incarceration than I am now.

This is so surreal that for a moment I wonder if I have fallen asleep in the projection booth and imagined the entire event.

This must be what Hannibal Lecter felt like. A padded cell is no place for such a brilliant mind! Incarceration has been documented on film so many times but by far my favourite is *The Shawshank Redemption*. Unfortunately there is no pickaxe or Rita Hayworth poster to help me get out of this mess. I really should be asleep in bed right now. I sit at the desk and assume that someone will be right with me. The minutes fly by in silence and I realise that my eyes are having a hard time adjusting to this bright room. In the distance I can hear patients and doctors talking. Some people go right past my door. I'll bet none of them even know I'm in here.

The police station is only a few minutes away. When two policemen come in I guess it's been at least twenty. I'm not a priority. The older cop sits opposite me while the younger one stands with a clipboard.

The older cop starts things off with a 'How's it going?'

'I'm alright… considering,' I offer. I wonder how many weeks from retirement he is.

'Do you want to tell us why we've been called out here tonight?'

I didn't call you. Why does he make it sound as if I'm wasting *his* time? I tell them the story of the cyclist riding in front of the car and my slamming on the brakes. The whole time I dart my eyes from one to the other and each time the younger cop is either taking notes or looking at me with disgust. I imagine all the mismatched police teams in film and television.

I imagine these two struggling to get along because of their age difference. For some reason it reminds me of the pairing of Chris Pine and Denzel Washington in *Unstoppable*. Perhaps a traumatic event will bring them closer together.

Maybe the younger cop will start dating his partner's daughter. That would be traumatic for the daughter. If he keeps giving me such a harsh stare he's going to give himself premature wrinkles.

'Is Lee alright?' I enquire after my explanation. I'm genuinely interested too. He was absolutely fine on the drive in and then collapsed in front of me. For a moment I wonder if he's dead.

'We're going to see him next.'

They have my official story now. The only real point of contention will be whether or not that road has a zebra crossing. When I told them about it I stressed that I was pretty sure I had the right of way. Lee assumed I was slowing down to let him walk.

Suddenly the image of Dustin Hoffman shouting *'I'm walking here! I'm walking here!'* leaps into my mind.

Before I know it I'm alone again in the brightest room in the world. It's so jarring to me to go from a darkened projection booth to this. Thinking back on the incident I wonder if I would have gotten away with just driving off. It would have been a hit and run. He wouldn't have caught my licence plate, I wouldn't have had to drive him to the hospital and I wouldn't be trapped here.

But what if he had collapsed by the side of the road? I'm now horrified by the idea that he is actually dead. Internal bleeding maybe? A sudden brain haemorrhage caused from the impact. During the interview I touched my face way too much. They'll think it's my 'tell' and that I'm guilty.

They return with the news that my story has been corroborated. Lee is fine. He was negligent and it wasn't a zebra crossing. I had the right of way! Amazingly the younger cop has relaxed his face. Maybe *this* is the event that has brought them closer together.

'We'll have to take some blood to make sure you don't have anything in your system but after that you'll be free to go.'

As I'm told this I feel a sudden relief. I'm innocent! Like Denzel in *The Hurricane*. Or Harrison Ford in *The Fugitive*. Of course my ordeal was only half an hour long but it was so intense and surreal that time seemed to slow down. The two policemen want to leave but they can't until someone comes in and takes a blood sample.

Eventually a different nurse comes in to do it. She's cute in a kind of 'authoritative woman in uniform' way and when she smiles at me the tiny room doesn't seem so bad. I don't love needles but I'm amongst the minority of the population that donates blood three to four times a year. When they first take your blood they tell you your blood type. If your blood type is common then you should donate more often because more people need that type.

It turns out I'm common.

I'm sure they just want everyone to donate more often. It can't hurt to have a healthy supply at the blood bank. I donate because I figure it's good karma and one day I might need it. I've never had a request like this one before. Giving blood to prove I'm *not* a drunk driver!

I ask about Lee and why he collapsed on the way into the hospital.

'Sometimes it only really hits people when they come through the doors. He probably became anxious and his body reacted.' The nurse tells me. 'He's fine though. That's sweet of you to ask.'

Blood is taken in front of the police to verify it's mine and then they say goodbye.

'Lee's bike is in the waiting room. Did you want me to bring it in for him?'

Even though I think I'm being chivalrous it falls on deaf ears. I'm ushered back towards the exit. They don't want me seeing him. I don't mind.

As I pass the nurse's station the woman that locked me in is sitting by the computer on the phone. She definitely sees me but I can't read her expression. It looks like she has moved on. I'm unimportant to her night. Just a task she had to complete earlier. She couldn't care less that I missed *Letterman*.

Then I stop in my tracks like I've been hit by a ton of bricks.

Sitting in the waiting room is the body of a model and the face of the girl next door. It's Alana! To her left is a guy in a grey singlet and jeans. He has the physique to make a singlet look good and immediately a wave of insecurity washes over me. Their body language is a dead giveaway. Fingers are interlocked. The look of joy on her face is one I'm unfamiliar with. This bozo is being cheated on too. *How did I not see it coming?* Alana is content to sit in this miserable room so long as she is with *this* guy. My new nemesis. He seems to have done something to his foot because he has crutches leaning against him. Probably rolled an ankle while they were running in slow motion toward each other in a field! I'm standing still and realise that I'm blocking someone from getting to the nurse's station. I walk out the door with purpose.

In the car I look at the back of the registration sticker on my windscreen and read the words for the first time. It says 'Watch out for cyclists.' It feels like I'm in *The Truman Show.*

I really am a bozo. Maybe I will go home and watch *High Fidelity* again.

A couple of weeks later I get a letter in the mail:

Dear Mr Charles Price,

RESULT OF ANALYSIS OF BLOOD SAMPLE:

On 23/02/2013 at 0115 hours a blood sample was taken from you by a member of our Medical team.

The result of the analysis of the blood sample is "ethyl alcohol was not detected in the sample."

The address where the sample of blood is being held is the A.C.T Government and Analytical Laboratory, 25 Mulley St, Holder, A.C.T 2611.

If you did not receive your sealed container of the sample of your blood at the hospital, an unanalysed sample of your blood may be obtained from the analyst within six months after the blood sample was taken, on your request or by another person authorised in writing by you to collect the blood sample.

Sincerely,

Patricia Healy

Blood and Breath Analysis Officer

TRAFFIC OPERATIONS

Great, now the government has my DNA on file. This is how cloning films start! The whole experience has a dreamlike quality for the next two weeks. The only proof of the accident is the puncture in my right arm and the letter. The first contact from Alana since that night is flashing on my phone a few weekends later.

Are you going out tonight? Give me a call.

I don't bother to respond. The 35mm film print of our love story was laced incorrectly and is scratched beyond repair. I hope that in the scheme of things Alana is such an insignificant part of my life that I'll forget her face completely one day soon.

A drunken text on a Friday night is meaningless.

I hate when girls use the excuse of being drunk to justify things like this.

Text me when you're sober!

Women know what they want and like to manipulate their way into getting it. I hope being cheated on can result in some great art for me. Maybe that's the upside of having been hurt. I'm filled with new ideas.

I turn on my computer and open a new blank document. Now I can start writing my killer projectionist screenplay.

Watch it at your own risk.

VHS

Luke's parents had finally caved last Christmas and given him a video camera after years of expressed interest. It was the most expensive and exciting toy he possessed and so naturally it travelled everywhere he did. It seemed second nature now for Luke to film his daily activities. He would see a dog or an interesting car and pop off his lens cap immediately. Melody was by far the most interesting person Luke had ever met which was probably why he felt the need to commit her to film.

As teenagers Luke and Melody became involved in the summer of 1991. It was a typical kind of adolescent infatuation. Melody had expressed an interest in Luke through various female confidants and the news had quickly reached Luke's tribe. It was far easier to ask a girl out in high school when you knew they already liked you and would definitely say yes. No girl had expressed any romantic interest in Luke before. His friends had dated a few girls and Luke had often wondered the particulars of how that all worked. Learning of her interest had destroyed any mystery that remained. Melody was the same height as Luke which was taller than average. Luke wondered if their perfectly matching height was a sign they were made for each other. He would look for signs in every conversation they had but they were few and far between.

Luke would point his camera at Melody and ask her questions. He wanted to know everything about her. She was such a beautiful soul.

Their growing relationship was always progressing towards sex and their loss of innocence. They were hands-on from day one and made every walk home from school last as long as possible. One day Melody had stopped and kissed Luke while they waited to cross the road. Luke held his breath and the kiss only ended due to his immediate need to exhale.

That summer Luke and Melody started to work their way through many intimate acts and grew closer every day. Despite the fact that neither of them had engaged in actual sex before Luke had devised a plan to ensure he would seem knowledgeable in his hour of need.

Luke's best friend Anthony worked in his uncle's video store most days after school. It was a pretty new enterprise that had sprung up after his uncle had seen Steven Soderbergh's *Sex, Lies and Videotape* and decided to invest in the growing industry of home entertainment. To celebrate this he had placed a large framed poster of *Sex, Lies and Videotape* behind the counter at the front of the store. Anthony was short, Italian and had a curiosity for women that stretched beyond his years. He and Luke would spend countless hours discussing women and the things they loved about them – or hoped to love. Often these conversations would be during a session of Super Nintendo at Anthony's parent's place where he would share his insights with his friend. After some pizza and ice cream one night Luke confided his trepidation towards taking the next step with Melody.

'I don't know what I'm doing really.'

'Seriously man?' Anthony sat up in his sleeping bag. Anthony had always been good about taking the floor when Luke slept over. 'You need to see this tape I have at the store. It will show you what to do.'

'What...like a film?'

'A porno, yeah.'

Luke was initially hesitant. He paused for longer than was socially acceptable before deciding that he *did* need guidance.

Anthony had a point: Pornography could be a teaching tool. It was time Luke learned how to be a man.

'Okay.'

'Okay? Nice one! I'm working tomorrow so I'll get it for you.'

And with that the plan solidified.

Luke was ready to watch the tape the following night. He was in the unique situation of having a second-hard VCR in his room, which made it much easier to avoid his parents. He couldn't imagine a more awkward situation than watching that tape with the people that had at one point in time wiped his bottom. He was a man now...or at least on the *cusp* of manhood. This was something he had to do alone. Luke turned the volume on his television down and put the tape in. The 'storyline' that followed involved a cameraman who was down on his luck and forced to start making porn. He then found himself both in front and behind the camera in a series of interludes. Luke had seen dirty magazines before but this was a sensory overload. The women came to life before his eyes. Suddenly Luke could see what all the fuss was about.

He took his camera and faced it towards the television set. He kept the volume low and made a crude copy of the tape. The next day he returned the original VHS to Anthony.

'So what did you think?'

'I've honestly never seen anything like it.'

'Let me know if you ever want to borrow it again.'

Luke thanked his friend but knew that it wouldn't be necessary. He had a copy of his own now.

About a week later Melody told Luke that she was ready to have sex with him. He turned red in the face.

'I'm ready too,' he said.

Alone in Luke's bedroom they started awkwardly undressed in front of each other. Luke suggested they get underneath the covers and Melody agreed. Eventually they found their stride. Neither made very much noise and when it was over the silence was overwhelming. Luke spoke first.

'Thank you.'

'What for?'

'That. It was…nice.'

'I liked it too. I'd been wanting to do that with you for a long time.'

'Me too.'

The two had sex at least four times a week from then on. Both parties were extremely willing to *practice* – as they dubbed it.

After a while Melody found the copied porno tape. Luke told her what it was and found himself surprised by her interest.

'Can I see it?'

'Sure.'

The two watched the pornography together and laughed at the faces the actors made. Melody asked him why he'd made a copy. Luke didn't know.

'Do you want to film…*us*?'

Luke had filmed everything since the moment he'd been given his camera. It made sense to film her too. He set up the camera on a tripod and pointed it at the bed. Melody and Luke made a twelve minute long sex tape.

'You can never ever show this to anyone Luke.'

'I won't.'

'Promise?'

'I promise.'

'This was just for us.'

Luke kept his word. He considered that since they made it together they would only ever watch it together.

After Christmas Melody's father got a new job and they moved away. Luke cried for days in the aftermath. His friend Anthony offered him pornography but he declined stating that he would 'never love again.' He tried to put the VHS tape – and Melody – out of his mind.

At first he thought about her every day.

Then she crossed his mind only a few times a week.

As the months went on it started to feel like a distant memory.

And then one day it felt like something that happened to someone else – and not to him at all.

He dated in college and put Melody and their summer together deep in the back of his mind. As technology advanced Luke got a DVD player. He grew up and got a job selling insurance plans. Luke bought a modest home and became engaged to a woman named Prue.

When his father died he went back to his family home to comfort his mother. It was during a cleanout of his old room that he rediscovered the tape. It was in a cardboard box with so many of his childhood memories. He couldn't believe that he had supressed that time with Melody.

Should he watch it? He'd never watched it then…would it be weird to watch it now? He'd promised himself that he would only watch it with Melody.

They were so young in the video that maybe watching it now would make him feel *dirty* somehow. He didn't even own a VCR anymore. He stored the box of memories in the cupboard and once again put Melody out of his mind.

He'd try to forget her all over again.

After a number of years Luke married Prue and started a family. He became involved with the minutiae of life. Buying socks, checking public transport timetables, making spaghetti and trying to stay in touch with his friends. His children loved their mother more than him but he didn't mind. Luke decided that winning their affection would be the challenge of his life.

It was years later – at the age of fifty-one – that he got a call from Anthony and was informed that Melody had died.

'How?'

'She was hit by a drunk driver. She was walking home apparently.'

Things seemed off balance for Luke.

As he hung up the phone he knew that a part of him was now dead too.

His wife didn't understand it and tried her best to let him grieve. He wanted to see Melody again and knew what he had to do. He purchased an old VCR and set aside a time when he would have the house to himself. It was a surreal feeling that he would finally revisit this moment in his life. He made a vow to watch the footage only once – as a means of saying goodbye – and then destroy the tape.

When Luke inserted the black cassette into the VCR and pressed play he saw his old bedroom. Memories came flooding back to him as he watched his younger self hop onto the bed. As Melody appeared in the frame Luke clasped his hand over his mouth. She smiled at the camera and it felt like the summer of 1991 all over again.

Time ceased to be for Luke as he was transported back to that moment. Before his life had really started to matter. Before responsibility and mortgages and children. He was innocent and stupid and young and happy.

Most of all he was in love with Melody.

How had he ever let her go?

Now that she was dead there would never be a reconciliation or a chance to tell her how much those days had meant. As Melody was undressing on the screen the VCR made a terrific mechanical noise and stopped playing the VHS tape.

Luke ejected it but it was too late. The tape had become frail over the years and had shredded inside the VCR.

It would never play again.

Luke curled up into a ball and wept. He didn't realise what he had. Luke had everything and he didn't know it. He was too young to know it.

It *was* real.

He knew that now.

It was the summer of 1991 that defined him. He *had* become a man after all.

He would stay with Prue and do his best to be a good father to their children. He would accept that his life was an enviable one and that he *should* be happy with his good fortune. If he could forget about Melody and pretend that Anthony never told him about her demise he could move forward with his life.

It was too late to change anything now.

Their time together had been short and they hadn't considered its importance. Luke had put everything about her in a box in his mind and sealed her away. Now he couldn't stop thinking about her.

But the tape wouldn't play ever again.

All Luke could do was mourn for his youth.

Melody was gone.

COMPANION

'I'm Lisa.'

'Nice to meet you Lisa. I'm Jackie...Jacqueline but everyone calls me Jackie.'

Lisa couldn't exactly place her accent but knew Jackie was American.

Lisa smiled and sat down on her bed. She felt the dark blue blanket and was pleased to find it was thick and probably quite warm. The room seemed to have a quiet and constant hum. There were no windows and she squinted as she analysed the artificial lighting.

'Has this been everything you hoped it would be?' Lisa asked her new companion.

Jackie sat down on the only other bed in the room. Her side was a mirror image of Lisa's. Jackie tied up her long black hair as she spoke.

'Look...if I'm being completely honest it's about what I expected. This room seems fine...and it's big enough for two. It's just a bit of an adjustment I suppose.'

Lisa nodded and wiped her palms from her thighs down to her knees. She had always felt nervous about meeting new people. She was intimidated by Jackie's confidence and beauty.

'So...do you like... blue?' she enquired.

It was something to say.

Something to fill the awkward silence.

Lisa regretted it immediately and worried about the kind of first impression she was making. She pointed at Jackie's clothes. 'Blue? Your tracksuit?'

'Oh this? I mean… I'll be cool in blue for now. They gave it to me – I didn't pick it. I'll get something else in a year. It doesn't really matter. I brought all my favourite clothes with me!'

Lisa picked up her own bag instinctively and placed it next to her on the bed.

'Did you sneak anything good in?' asked a curious Jackie.

'No… just some family photos. Nothing that wasn't allowed.'

'Too bad.'

Lisa, still feeling uncomfortable, decided to do a lap of her new surroundings. The beds were on one side of the room while the other had been divided into a bathroom, shower and small kitchenette. There was a computer screen near the light switch that appeared to be off. There were four small red lights in the corners of the room that Lisa assumed were cameras.

'Have you been waiting for me long?' she asked Jackie as she slid open each kitchen storage space for inspection. There were various snacks in each drawer. It looked a bit like a hotel mini bar.

'Not really. I've had about an hour to myself. Glad you finally made it though.'

'There was a bit of a line-up,' Lisa offered by way of apology.

'It's all good. So is purple *your* favourite colour?' Jackie asked indicating at Lisa's jumpsuit.

'Yes.'

'That's great! See…we're getting to know each other already.'

The accent was bothering Lisa. It was so familiar too.

'Where are you from Jackie?'

'Forth Worth, Texas. How about you?'

'Ah that's the accent. I'm from Singapore. My parents moved there from Australia when I was young.'

'Did you like it there?'

'It was very clean.'

Jackie smiled, showing off her very white teeth. 'Do you have a boyfriend back in Singapore Lisa?'

'No.'

'A girlfriend then?'

'No.'

'Did you have a family pet? Come on Lisa, gimme something here! I'm trying to get to *know* you.'

'Sorry,' she replied meekly. 'I had a goldfish.'

Jackie's face fell.

'*Fascinating*,' she said sarcastically.

'Um...there isn't much to say really. I'm here because Yuri Wang recruited me himself. He read some essays I wrote on botany. I also dabble in biology.'

'That's your *resume*. I wanted to get to know your personality. We're going to be spending a lot of time together and I figured it would be better spent if we got along.'

'Of course... sorry Jackie. Tell me about your life in Texas?'

'Well! I was one of five children – all older brothers – and I went to Texas Christian University. I was in a Sorority there…do you know what that is? A Sorority?'

'Yes.'

'Well they have them at Christian Universities too… I was a bit of a party girl….*Wooooo!* My sisters and I used to rule the school. I dated the wide receiver on the football team for a while…he wanted to marry me but I wasn't in love with him…I was a cheerleader in my first year there but it was too much of a commitment. I liked drinking too much I suppose. Training – even cheerleader training – is very taxing on the body, don't you know?'

Lisa studied Jackie. She was her polar opposite. While Lisa felt introverted and studious Jackie presented herself as social and extroverted. Lisa wondered what she was doing here as she had neglected to mention any special skills besides drinking.

'Did I tell you I brought my cheerleading outfit?' she continued.

Lisa shook her head as she struggled to get a word in edgewise.

'It's so cute. You'll love it. I still remember *all* the cheers. If you want I can teach you some of my moves?'

'Maybe.'

'Did you leave your parents behind?' asked Jackie as she moved into the kitchenette.

'Yes. They were very understanding.'

'Good, good. Mine were *not!* They were pissed off.'

'Why?'

'They've always been angry with me... I was the baby of the family and I guess being the only girl they didn't know what to do with me. My dad was a drinker and he was kind of violent too. I used to run away a lot...I guess I'm still kind of running away.'

Lisa looked at the ground because the exchange felt too personal. It was so early and she wasn't ready for this kind of honesty. She said nothing and started to unpack her bag into a small set of drawers next to her bed. Jackie hovered over to inspect the contents of Lisa's bag.

'You brought books?'

'Yes. I like to read,' replied Lisa.

'They have a digital library here though. You didn't need to bring those.'

'I like the feel of having a book in my hands. And these ones have sentimental value to me.'

'Weird,' replied Jackie.

Lisa unpacked a handful of knick-knacks from her home in Singapore. She decided not to take out her photo album in case Jackie wanted to discuss each picture. Jackie seemed bored by the contents of Lisa's bag. She skipped across the room to her bag and started to pull item after item out enthusiastically. When she found her old cheerleader outfit she squealed with delight.

'Here it is! You've got to see this on me! It's soooooo cute.'

Jackie pulled down her blue tracksuit pants and unzipped and removed her jacket. She threw them down on her bed casually before picking up and admiring her cheerleader outfit once again. Her underwear was tight and black. Without her tracksuit to conceal them Lisa counted three tattoos on Jackie's person. She wondered if there were any more hidden away. Jackie caught Lisa staring and smiled widely as she dressed herself.

'What do you think?'

'Sorry…I didn't mean to…'

'It totally fine!' Jackie said quickly. 'The whole reason I got fake breasts was so that people would look at them.'

Lisa could feel herself blushing.

'The guys back in Texas said I used to be a ten but with these boobs I'm now a *twelve*!' she proclaimed proudly.

When Jackie was dressed she started to dance around the room in a rehearsed manner. All she was missing was a set of pom poms.

'Jackie?'

'Yeah?'

'Why are you here?'

'What do you mean?' asked Jackie.

'Why are you here on the transport vessel? I don't mean to be rude but what are your skills? Why were you of all people selected to join the new colony?'

Jackie looked offended for only a moment. She did a quick shrug and answered.

'I'm a breeder. I'm told I'm a good physical specimen…no history of mental illness. I mean… *Yuri Wang* didn't personally select me or anything but I'm here…as you put it…to make babies and relieve sexual tension.'

Lisa's face curled up. The idea of prostitution was revolting to her.

'Relax Lisa. It's not like I'll be bringing men back *here* or anything. There are zones on the ship for that.'

'I...don't mean to judge you. I apologise.'

'Are you like...a virgin or something Lisa? You can tell me. I knew lots of virgins at University.'

'No. I'm not.'

'Okay...so you've had sex?'

'Yes.'

'So you know it's not a big deal.'

'I'm sorry but...I believe it *is* a big deal.'

'Are you worried I might get pregnant? Relax! I'm *supposed* to get pregnant. I've got to repopulate the colony and all that.'

Lisa wanted to leave the room but she knew it was impossible. She had to remain in isolation with Jackie for the next two years as the spaceship travelled to the new colony. She plugged noise-cancelling earplugs into her ears and pulled her dark blue blanket up to her neck. Lisa faced away from Jackie and went to sleep. She found her new companion's inane chatter suffocating.

When she woke up Lisa had no idea how much time had passed. There were no clocks to measure it. She sat up and looked over to Jackie.

Lisa saw that while she had been asleep her roommate had rummaged through her bag. Lisa's photo album and her books were all opened on Jackie's bed. She was livid. She *hated* Jackie.

'Jackie! How could you? Why did you go through my bag?'

There was no reply.

'Jackie?'

Lisa approached Jackie and saw that she had been eating snacks in bed. There were crumbs all over the books that her father had given her as a farewell gift. There were also various nuts scattered on the front of Jackie's blue jumpsuit.

'Jackie? Are you alright?'

She was dead.

Jackie had been throwing cashews into the air and catching them in her mouth. She'd allowed one to bounce into her windpipe and Jackie had choked to death as Lisa slept.

A fingerprint scanner lit up next to the bed. Lisa was familiar with the technology. Yuri Wang had devised a series of these fingerprint panels for the occupants of this transport vessel. They served as a means of 'checking in' with everyone on board. Everyone that resided in the ship would need to touch their fingers to the panel on a daily basis to advise the crew that they were safe in their quarters. It was an automated system. It was protocol.

Lisa pressed her outstretched fingers against the panel by her bed. She then took Jackie's limp palm and gently twisted it up to the second panel. The light turned from red to green. Lisa let Jackie's hand fall as she brushed the crumbs from her belongings.

Lisa embraced the silence.

STRANGE

There it was in black and white: *Film Crew Wanted*. I'd always wanted to make a movie. It didn't really matter what role I played in the production – I just wanted to be there.

This would be my first screen credit. From what I could glean the film looked like it was about a teenager who had visions or fantasies. A single crude poster wasn't much to go on.

The Director was the one who answered my email. He simply replied:

What position on the crew do you want to do?

I had no idea and told him as much. I assumed I would be holding a boom microphone for hours at a time. He suggested *First Assistant Director*, which basically meant I would be second in command. It was an honour considering I didn't know what I was doing. I had almost no experience in the craft of filmmaking at all. The Director and I did have the same first name though. This fact meant he could call me 'Number Two' on set. He seemed to enjoy it even though at times I felt it was akin to calling me 'shit.'

I was just grateful to be there at the end of the day. I wasn't in a position to complain and I had been welcomed with open arms. I didn't ask him for his credentials and he didn't ask me for mine.

I later learned that he'd been a child star in New Zealand although no footage of his acting ever surfaced. I didn't know if he was lying or exaggerating the truth. I told him I'd co-hosted a morning cartoon show once – which was true – but it was because I'd won a competition, not because I was a talented host. The whole experience had been awful and I'd disliked seeing myself on screen.

He didn't want to be in front of the camera either. He was playing the part of Director. This *was* the performance.

He was living it and everyone was buying it. In a way they didn't have as much on the line. If the film was a success – they were a part of it. If it failed they could easily distance themselves from it. The Director has the most ownership of a film. It's their vision at the end of the day.

The crew assembled and we met at his residence, which we learned he shared with his mother. The hierarchy between them was quickly established – it was *her* house but she seemed happy to support this creative endeavour.

There were many accomplished people in that group. Some had travelled to be there too. In hindsight they were more committed than they should have been. Everyone had more experience than me but the nature of my role meant that all I had to do was account for time. I was to run the schedule and make sure we got the job done. I thought it would be easy enough to stick to a schedule if everyone was doing their job. In truth we were all learning as we went along and learning can be time consuming.

The Director seemed to think that if he spoke his dream out loud - the universe would provide. I'd asked to see the script and been told to be patient.

I tried to be. I felt like a 'yes man.' I kept telling people that the film was going to be good because that was the narrative I was being fed. In truth I had no idea.

The crew grew and the casting began. He was soon surrounded by people with starry eyes and wide smiles. Everyone saw it as an opportunity. We continued to meet and hang out but nobody could move forward until the script was officially finished.

In truth nobody saw a word until it was too late. We'd all committed ourselves to the project. Then the day finally came.

It wasn't a terrible script. It was a *rushed* script. The sustained rumour was that his mother had written large chunks of it. It was also saddled with the disappointing ending that 'it was all a dream.' This twist ending devalued everything that came before it. None of the events in the movie actually mattered because they were all taking place inside the lead character's head.

We did a read through inside a demountable building that had been rented for rehearsals by the Director. The only rehearsals I'd witnessed until now were acting exercises that felt made up on the spot. I had photographed some of these 'rehearsals' to document the behind the scenes action but the cast were getting restless. People were sick of meeting up and flailing around. They wanted to see the script as much as I did. Cast members were asking *me* when the script would be available. I had no idea until the Director surprised us with it. Now – armed with a script – I thought we would finally achieve something.

I was wrong.

The read through was met with a lacklustre response. The Director was not open to improving the script and wanted his words left alone. It was done as far as he was concerned. We had to move on to the next phase. He was the leader and we respectfully followed his wishes. It was full steam ahead.

The Director told us that although he couldn't afford to pay us anything up front that each of us was entitled to 1% of the films earnings at the end.

The lead actor dropped out but it didn't take long to fill the role. There was a plethora of bodies that had been attending the rehearsals under the impression that they would all appear as students in the classroom scenes. Most of them didn't get any screen time in the end.

During Production I learned lots of basic filmmaking techniques like 'crossing the line.' If two actors faced each other and you imagined an invisible line between them you needed to stay on one side of that invisible line while shooting their coverage. If you didn't by the time you came to edit the scene the shots wouldn't cut together. Both actors would be facing the same way instead of appearing to interact with each other. I gobbled up these simple lessons and through osmosis found myself having a great time.

The twelve day shoot blew out to sixteen days. Suddenly it was every weekend. It became a second job for most of us. It was exhausting and one by one people became unavailable. Scheduling became more difficult. On set morale slipped and smoke breaks increased. My role started to meld into that of a personal assistant. When lunchtime was approaching I picked it up and delivered it to set. I was ok with it. I was *still* just happy to be there.

I made friends with actors and have a vivid memory of singing *Backstreet Boys* while riding in the passenger seat of the lead actor's car. In my position I was also in charge of all of the extras on set. I gave them direction and tried to make the background action as interesting and alive as possible without stealing focus from the main story. I invited my curious friends to come and act as extras during a nightclub scene. They quickly saw through the Director and were happy when they could leave.

How did they see what I could not?

The day we had blood squibs placed under the actors clothing by a professional armourer was a huge day. This professional that had worked on hundreds of memorable

Australian films was gracing us with his presence. The squibs were easily the greatest part of the whole shoot. That day – which was one of the last days – felt the most like we were on a *real* film set.

Of course there were still many scenes to go. Nobody realised that we were blowing holes in the actor's costumes until it was too late.

I had to go to the mall during my lunch break and buy new tops. It was a weird scavenger hunt but I found all three actors replacement clothing in less than an hour. We should have thought ahead.

There were times on set where I took his side. I didn't need to and I didn't make any friends because of it but that was the debt I owed him. I was his right hand man and that meant agreeing with him. Once I remember trying to push everyone to do just *one* more scene and sleep in the next day. The crew united and refused to go on. They were all tired of filmmaking.

One of the final days of shooting took place inside a school. We'd already set off the school's fire alarm accidently and lost an hour while we waited for the fire department to come and go. The Director was feeling nostalgic. He wanted to do something memorable and bond us all together. Naturally he suggested that all of the male members of the cast and crew go streaking through the halls of the high school.

Nobody went for it and he didn't want to do it alone. Even as his yes man this was not something I could say yes to.

Whenever something went awry the catchphrase became 'we'll fix it in post.' The job of the editor was quickly becoming a monumental task. The Director would later state that his editor *saved* the film. I can only imagine what the first cut looked like.

As continuity became a problem, issues were waved away.

'It's all a dream, remember? So we can just put it down to that.'

Nothing mattered.

When it was all finally over we had a big wrap party to celebrate. It took place at the Director (and his mother's) house. It was at this party that many of the cast and crew hooked up with one another. Was this the point all along?

I decided to put the whole thing down as a learning experience and move on. I still wanted to create and so I started working on my own screenplay.

After about nine months the Director was in touch again. He wanted to play the film for me and my girlfriend at the time. I invited him to come over and screen the film that weekend. I set up my television so that the VCR was recording the DVD output. I hadn't seen anything from that shoot. I wanted to watch the film and analyse it. I knew that would be impossible. He would never *willingly* leave me a copy. I had to covertly make my own.

We watched the film together and in the middle he insisted on an intermission so that he could have a cigarette. It made the VHS recording I was making far less watchable in the months to come. There was now a ten-minute freeze frame in the middle of it that I had to fast forward whenever I reviewed the footage.

It was interesting to see the footage cut together but it wasn't ground breaking. Parts of it felt like I was watching a home movie. In terms of the craft of filmmaking some things were shot badly. There was a chase scene that could have been great but felt comical instead.

None of the characters grew or changed or had emotional arcs during the film. I expressed my congratulations that he'd finished it. I was glad it was all coming to an end and we could move on. My girlfriend at the time wasn't very impressed. The Director took this opportunity – out of nowhere - to state that because the film was set in a dream state that we would be *reshooting* additional scenes to 'pump up' the film. He wasn't here to show me a finished version of the film at all – he was here to recruit. In my opinion his sequences sounded like fun and I agreed to help.

If nothing else it would be a good chance to see the cast and crew again. My girlfriend disagreed. She told me that filmmaking was a waste of my time and it was a contributing factor in our eventual breakup.

It was a while before we shot the additional scenes. They were an assortment of random fight scenes – including a Kung-Fu fight *and* a boxing match – a chase scene and several sexually charged moments that would serve to make the film seem more interesting. The Director had also convinced two girls to kiss each other on camera. The trailer started to get attention online.

On the night of the premiere we saw his vision realised. All of the hard work was collected into a 96 minute feature that was presented to us all.

He spoke before the film and thanked us. It was brief but sincere. He couldn't have done it without us. Either way his dream was coming true.

There was a title card at the beginning of the film. That was new. It acted as an apology for what the audience was about to watch. It informed the cinema that the film was made by amateurs and should be forgiven for any faults. It was riddled with spelling mistakes too.

The movie started with a montage of dancing intercut with a scene of assault.

It was an odd juxtaposition. It was unclear who the main character was for the first ten minutes of the film.

When the actual movie began the dialogue was buried under music during vital moments. Exposition was lost.

All of the additional scenes we shot were jarringly inserted into the film. It was strange and there wasn't much connective tissue holding the plot together. Improvised scenes in the classroom seemed to dominate the film. They were overlong and ultimately irrelevant. It felt more tedious and boring than actual school classes ever could.

While they were editing, the Director and his editor had been bored with the film. In their state of boredom they had dubbed over one actor's lines and inserted their own rambling *Blah Blah Blahs*. The only problem was that neither had thought to remove this joke from the final cut. It made no sense to the audience at all.

I had watched sections of the film multiple times over having bootlegged it months earlier. This gave me a chance to reflect on what I was watching. Women were treated badly in the film. In one scene – for no reason – a male character spat at a female character. The story boiled down to a mother and son relationship. Did it mirror the Director's relationship with his mother? I tried to read between the lines but it was unclear what the film was trying to say.

An attempt to stitch together two unrelated scenes resulted in laughs from the crowd. The film was unintentionally hilarious like Tommy Wiseau's *The Room*. The audience didn't know why none of the characters ever changed clothes and by the end they didn't care. The twist 'dream' ending was too little too late. In the end the film was too unfocused.

It had started with an average script and resulted in an average independent film. The result was a polite applause and a hasty exit. The film was trashed online and the Director was exhausted. Years had been put into that project.

He listed his film into all of the databases he could but he marketed the film very strangely. He told everyone verbally and in print that the budget was less than a million dollars.

This was true, of course, as the budget was probably closer to fifteen thousand dollars. The downside of such a brag meant that people thought they were getting a production of blockbuster standards.

I couldn't help but wonder if this was a way of making sure none of us got our *1% of the profits* deal. If he claimed the budget was a million dollars then it would have to make a million dollars before it was in profit. It was destined to make nothing.

When I finally got my own personal copy of the film it boasted the quote 'The independent film of the year' but did not attribute the quote to anyone. The word independent had also been misspelled on the cover. He hadn't changed a thing from the night of the premiere. He'd even left in the *Blah Blah Blahs*. Just because you claim you are a filmmaker it doesn't make it true. Just as claiming the film was the 'best independent film' didn't make it true. He seemed to be living in a strange fantasy world.

In the aftermath of the production he convinced me that I should write a script *with* him. This was based on the assumption that I knew what I was doing as I had churned out a semi-suspenseful screenplay called *The Stranger* during the period of time that he had been editing the film. I found it funny that he wanted to make a *different* film – one on which *he* was the cowriter – rather than help me make *The Stranger*. I didn't love the idea of a second collaboration but I did like the idea of seeing my words performed on screen. I wanted to build up my screen credits and experience. Maybe with the same enthusiasm he could help me get my film made. I found out very quickly that I was still to be 'Number Two' on this project.

The film was to be titled *Authenticity* and it centred on a girl's first few months at University. He pitched grand ideas of toga parties and a character called Minx that would always be dressed in different clothes.

I countered by claiming it would work as a love story where perhaps she meets someone unexpected and a rom-com unfolds. We met somewhere in the middle and I commenced writing.

After forty pages of work I supplied my script in progress to my new writing partner. I provided them as physical pages and not in any format he could manipulate without me. He printed a new cover – one that put his name first despite a severe lack of input – and tucked the forty pages into a binder. He gave notes and criticised my words. It was fine. My skin was thicker this time around. I let the weeks pass and predictably he wrote nothing. I asked him for pages and he avoided me.

He created another mock up poster for the film – the tag line read: *Coming of age has never been so real!* It didn't even make sense to me. He wanted to do auditions for the film, claiming that it helped his way of writing to have an actor in mind. It was a cop out. He put up YouTube videos stating that the film was 'cutting edge' and 'a coming of age story with balls.' His videos ended by asking people to submit their auditions by December as the film would be shooting 'early next year.' I caved and we did the auditions. Maybe this really was part of the process for him. It had been the case on the previous feature. It was sad to see how many people were dragged out to audition for a project that didn't exist yet. I dutifully videotaped each one for posterity.

Although I kept asking, no pages materialised from him. I decided the best thing to do was to stop asking. I waited and he lost interest in the project. This would be the theme for years.

I followed his exploits online. Each year he re-invented himself and claimed some new project he was starting. Each time he created a crude poster to lure people into thinking the film was real. They were ambitious and expensive ideas. Sometimes he started a website so he looked more legitimate. He had the vision but he no longer had a band of willing helpers. They had lost faith in him.

At one point he reached out to me with the intention of having me work on his film but I was now living in another state and didn't want to come back.

For a while he dropped off the radar. We had a chat when he surfaced. It had been twelve years since we'd met on that first feature film. I was conducting interviews for a podcast and wanted to interview him about our shared experience. I wanted to get some answers for myself and hear the stories from his point of view. I convinced him to do an audio commentary for his film. It was a great chance for me to get him on the record for 96 minutes. Was I remembering things incorrectly? Was there a perfectly logical explanation for everything that had happened?

He agreed to record it with me. He casually told me that he'd be able to do it that weekend and then cancelled on me. He rescheduled and left me in the lurch a second time. The third time he informed me that he should be 'fine to do it' but if he didn't respond to my text that he was most likely in jail. He'd broken the conditions of his parole and had to appeal for his freedom in court. Though in the end he was able to stay out of prison I was never able to record the audio commentary with him. He remained elusive and I was no closer to getting answers. I decided to stop asking him about it.

Last year he claimed he would shoot *three* feature films in as many months. He told me he would edit the films while they were being shot and have a first cut to play for the cast and crew at the wrap party.

It was too much. Instead of focusing on one film at a time he told me that he was 'great at scheduling' and could make all three 'no problem.'

He was coming off as delusional.

It had started as a fun adventure. It was about telling a story and making something. Now it was about proving a point. He was struggling with his *"difficult second album."* He told me he'd been working on his craft and was better at Directing.

He told me he'd been to film school although he never used the word *graduated*. The Director was trying to do too much. He was like a sculptor on a conveyer belt abandoning projects after spending only a moment with them. He moved on too quickly to make anything worthwhile. I was confident *none* of these film ideas would see the light of day but I tried to be enthusiastic.

I wanted to offer the same lifeline he had once offered me. But his timeframe was insane. He had completely blocked out how long a single feature film had taken him. He was like a mother that immediately forgot the pain and ordeal of childbirth.

As expected he abandoned all three films.

He changed his name. The rumour was that he had to disappear in order to avoid all of the money he owed people. I'd heard that he never paid for the rehearsal space in that demountable building. I couldn't be sure if it was true. He changed his name back. Apparently a porn star had become famous off the new moniker and it was no longer original.

When I think of the movie we made, or I'm silly enough to re-watch it, I try to remember that back then it didn't really matter what role I played in the production – I just wanted to be there. I hope that one day he sits down and writes just *one* screenplay. I hope he shows it to his mother and his friends and then – based on their input – *revises* the story. I hope that he thinks about his film long before he decides to make a cruce poster for it or assemble a hopeful cast and crew. I hope the Director works again because it would be a shame if that one film was his legacy.

I think he has more to say than that. His own life story is more interesting than the fictional name he's been trying to make for himself. I don't think that his story is over but I guess time will tell.

THE AIRPORT

What if the outfit you're going to die in is already hanging in your wardrobe?

I'm dying.

We're all dying I suppose but I'll be dead much sooner than most.

I'm dying but this is my chance to leave a legacy. These are my final days and my final thoughts. Is it important to give you the full picture of my life? Perhaps all the sordid details would be best. This will serve as the most honest reflection of who I was in life, and should be read only after my death. If you find yourself with this in your hand I have most likely perished. That sounds unreal to me, as if I am expired milk or something.

I will introduce myself first - I'm Markus. I won't give you my last name as I don't want the tale of my life to be fact checked *too* closely but I will say that I feel like a fraud right now. I hardly read anything in school and to now attempt to write my own story seems wrong, especially since I have no particular achievement to my name. I never excelled in sport or academics and had an attention span that forced me to change hobbies with the seasons. It's bizarre what a tumour will do to put things in perspective.

I found out three weeks ago that I have an inoperable tumour in my head. Fuck I hate doctors. Now more than ever! I went through all the stages you're supposed to. I thought all about my life and the things I would never get to do.

I cried until I felt nothing.

I am absolutely afraid of dying.

When I was nine years old I nearly died by choking on chewing gum while riding a bike so I guess you could argue that I got thirty extra years.

I find it odd to think about the things I wanted and the things I want now. I find myself longing to go to Disneyland and get a bunch of cheesy photos with my childhood idols. Anything to take my mind off the inevitable end. The adult in me wishes I had invented something. That way I would have more of a legacy to be remembered by. I think it would have been cool to have had a drink named after me. Something alcoholic and easy to make. I have no idea what, and that really goes to show why 'the Markus' doesn't exist. I can imagine ordering a 'Markus' from the bar and getting a blank stare.

Yesterday I looked through all the recent photos of myself trying to pick one for display at my funeral. I hated every picture more than the last. I look like a happy and oblivious idiot.

My day job – which in retrospect consumed too much of my time – was manager of a bank downtown from my home. I was the model employee too. I wore an ironed suit and tie almost every day of my working life. I started at the bottom and proved my way to the top. Of course I always had a boss. Not having one would have put me to blame when things went wrong. I was a soldier, not a general.

Why didn't I have the kind of job where I got more time off? Or even one where I didn't have to shave everyday. I only grew a beard once in my life on a dare. I wanted to do it though. What man doesn't want to sport a beard and be a man? My memories of my job are all a blur. Infinite days of numbness. The income at the management level was sufficient that I was not *unhappy*, merely unstimulated. It was the kind of income where you got comfortable and didn't want to leave your post.

I really don't know what to write. How terrible is that? That my life isn't worth putting on paper.

There must be something. I'll take a break and come back.

Alright.

I have cause to note two occasions that I feel worthy of recollection. In May of last year I helped the most grateful single mother to afford her second home. Her first was sold for less than it was worth following a divorce. The husband was making a home with his new lover and she found herself pregnant with his child. A parting gift. Helping this woman in need was almost worth the nineteen years of pseudo slavery. The second most prominent memory – and one that happened in my first year of banking - was coming to work only minutes after the bank was robbed. I had missed the entire thing. I think the thing about that situation that stayed with me was the look in the eyes of everyone who was there. They had been through something that morning. Fear is a powerful driver. I wish I could experience something other than fear now. I am glad I missed that robbery. I heard that the two robbers held machetes up to the necks of the tellers. A few of them had minor injuries after being roughed up and threatened.

I just overslept that morning.

The bank wasn't my first job though. I packed shelves at a toy store and then at a supermarket. I look back on those days as the most carefree of my existence. I drove a blue Toyota Corolla that had a tiny hole in the floor. You could see the road flying by as you drove. It was visible out of the corner of your eye. I remember getting the car cheaply and as time went by the hole getting slowly bigger. The weird thing was that I had to get rid of the car because its engine blew up and was going to cost more than the car was worth. I truly thought that the hole would get too big and take the car down somehow. It was like having a tumour grow slowly, threatening to kill the host, and then instead the host getting hit by a car. The engine failing came out of nowhere.

I just fucking *love* surprises. Don't you?

I guess I have looked at a lot of photos since the diagnosis. I think I only have my earliest memories because of how much I have looked at my infant self. I don't remember any of the events in the pictures but they must have happened. I wish I *could* remember. It feels like a part of my life that happened to someone else. I guess this whole tale is like those photos. If I don't take note of my life it will be like it never happened. I have to capture it.

I guess the first real memory I have is when I was a toddler. I remember ruining Christmas. My parents constantly retold this story to relatives and friends throughout my teens. I think back fondly on their version of events as I found it comforting to think they enjoyed the experience as much as I did.

The day started like every Christmas before it. I was a child and still cried at odd hours. Waking my parents allowed me access to the lounge room where the presents sat patiently under the tree. Not knowing their significance I was left alone long enough to unwrap present after present. I couldn't tell you why I was left unattended for so long. Maybe my parents fell asleep somewhere. Maybe they were exchanging presents of their own. Regardless, when my mother returned to collect me I was nowhere to be found. Instead she stood face to face with a pile of wrapping and several exposed gifts. Thankfully I had left a trail. My mother proceeded to follow one lolly wrapper after another until she saw me sitting under the stairs, surrounded by wrappers and the remains of a present from my cousins. I had a thing about sweets it would seem. This haunted me throughout my days. I'm sure I will recall multiple times here that I took something sweet and squandered it.

I should write about Sally. I truly hope she gets her hands on a copy of this and knows how I really felt. I think she knows. The last time I saw her was so many years ago. I was a few years into my job as a teller and went to see her.

We hadn't been together for a while and I thought that the job was going to help us get over the issues we had. Things that kept us apart I guess.

She was with someone else but I didn't think it was serious. Sally wouldn't do anything to hurt me. The truth, unfortunately, was that she had moved on. Betrayal is an ugly thing and I reacted in an ugly way. Not only did I fly off the handle but I think I damaged our relationship beyond repair. I couldn't be the bigger man. I couldn't walk away. I know looking back that proposing wasn't the right thing to do. Women want proposals to be big and at the height of the relationship. They don't want to be courted on an angry ultimatum. What I can remember of it only makes me upset.

I don't *get* women. I think all men pretend to, but none of us really *get* women. I had a sister growing up. She was four years older and did all the rebellious things that I wish I could do. She took the fun out of things I guess. After she got busted with drugs I got to see how mad it made my parents. I didn't see what the point was. I didn't want to do anything to hurt them. My sister Melissa did countless things to stir them up. She threatened to run away, threatened to drink drive. She rebelled until there was nothing left for me to do. I think maybe as a result I did nothing.

The truth is, here at age thirty-nine, I'm alone. I need to go back and sift through things to work out what went wrong. Or *did* it go wrong? Was my life considered a success? I don't even know. All I know is that life should be longer than thirty-nine years. While I should be having a midlife crisis I am looking at the end of the line. I have never been afraid of death because I never thought I would be told when it was coming. I'm fucking scared shitless now though.

The problem with doing this kind of 'mental stocktake' is that I keep thinking that the next thing I write will be the *last* thing I write.

It's weird but it kind of motivates me to keep going as I re-read what I wrote and think *I have more to say*. It is a horrible feeling not knowing how this transcript will end. I *want* to have more to say. I really want more time.

I feel guilty about all the bad things I have done and regret about all the things I never got to do. I have no faith in mankind. I only hope that someone will read this and see what I was like. Maybe they'll find the humanity in what I have been through. I want to be remembered. That seems selfish when I write it down. Maybe the people in these stories from my life will read them and remember and laugh. I read once that you die twice: once when your body dies and once the last time your name is spoken out loud. I think I'll be remembered by those I loved. For a while anyway.

I love women. I will probably always regret not taking more chances with them. Companionship was never something I thought about before three weeks ago. I never really owned a pet except for a fish when I was young. If I had a dog now and I died in my home then it might not be found for days. I don't have regular visitors and I have requested solitude to get my thoughts down on paper. If nobody visited for days then my theoretical dog may take to eating me as an alternative to starving. I have never thought about becoming a cannibal. I suppose I was always too repulsed by the idea. What if I was in a small plane crash? The kind of plane that carried twelve passengers or so. I'm isolated, have no means of communication, limited supplies, and there are several fresh corpses right there. With no sign of rescue and time passing I *still* don't think I could do it. I don't value my life enough to be remembered as the guy who ate the man from seat 2B.

I keep thinking about Sally. If I had to guess I would say she got married because she's not on Facebook under her own name. Maybe she died. That's a horrible thought. I smoked my first cigarette with Sally and the image of her blowing smoke at me is burned in my mind. The best thing about a woman who smokes is that she's not afraid to put something bad in her mouth. Sally and I would spend time together after school. We shared our first ash flavoured kiss under a tree where we sat one afternoon. I told her it wasn't my first kiss but it actually was. She was special. I thought - when we were all over each other that day - Sally and I would be together forever.

I spent a whole week's pay setting up our night to remember. I booked a hotel room nearby. It had a spa. I let my imagination run wild as I paid for it. I felt the stares of the women at the counter as I, at age sixteen, was barely legally able to rent the room. Come to think of it – I have no idea how old you have to be to check yourself into a hotel room for one night only. Maybe it's eighteen? I think she gave me the keys because I looked a bit older than I was.

I have always looked a bit older.

This has helped me in life. I was able to talk to girls who may have been a bit older than me and a bit more experienced. Although if I have always looked older have I been ageing faster than most? What if this tumour shouldn't have become a tumour so soon and the only reason I have it is because of my accelerated growth. I have never heard of this as a condition but what if I'm the first? I suppose it would be hard to test for. The tumour might just be from years of TV and computer screens and mobile phone use. I'll never know.

I had to put down a ridiculous deposit to get the key to the hotel room that night. Sally had a curfew and had to be home at a certain time. I told her about the idea a week before. I was excited for our first time. Sex is something that I had wondered about in quiet fascination. Sally was the perfect person to try it with. She'd had sex before. When the time came I waited patiently for her in the hotel room. I watched TV and sat on the bed. She arrived in a summery dress that I immediately wanted to look under. She was beautiful.

The problem was after I had her there I froze. I took her on a tour of the room, which consisted of a large bathroom with a spa in the centre, and a balcony with ashtrays. What happened next I cannot explain.

We sat down on the bed and watched TV. It wasn't particularly interesting, as I cannot recall what was on. I didn't initiate anything and neither did she. I thought once you get a beautiful woman into a place alone things would just click. After I had all the components though - it fell flat. The evening wore on and we didn't even kiss. I guess I figured at some stage she would have taken charge considering she had done this kind of thing before and seeing as how I had made all the plans and effort.

Nothing.

At the end of our time Sally went home. I had entered the hotel room with every intention of staying the night. I had briefed my parents with a well set up back story that had been dropped into every possible conversation for the last week. I stood alone in the room and contemplated using the spa. I decided against it, called a taxi and went home. The room was left unused in every way despite my best intentions. I never even used the bathroom.

She told me later that she was sorry, which confirmed that maybe she had done something wrong, and that she *did* want to have sex with me - just maybe not in a hotel room like that. I had looked at our situation and found that as underage students who still lived with their parents we had no other place to go. To me the hotel room was the best idea and I had hastily spent all my money. Following the events of the hotel room, or lack thereof, I put the whole relationship into autopilot. I stopped trying and said stupid things to her. I resented her for that night.

Over time Sally probably just got tired of my shit. After we went our separate ways the idea of being with her stayed with me. I think you are less picky when you first take an interest in women, as everything is new. That's probably why most people don't marry the first person they kiss. We're all just a mess of hormones at the start.

I didn't see her for years. After school ended we each signed a yearbook and hugged in a way that suggested we would see each other all the time. We didn't though. I rarely took to smoking after that. I dabbled with weed and had a cigar when my good friend Joe had a baby but mostly I just thought about Sally whenever I smelt smoke. I guess the lingering smell was like her perfume.

We ran into each other in our twenties and started to date. It was the happiest I'd ever been.

She was focussed and determined to build me into the man that *she* wanted for herself. At least that is how I perceived it at the time. As I viewed it back then she was trying to change me. She had a rich family and they bought her a house. She asked me if I wanted to move in with her. Sally wanted me to pay half the rent. I felt suffocated. I saw all the negative parts of it instead of the positives. I looked at her parents and imagined Sally repeating all their moves. Her mother had dated a *stud* of a man – her words not mine – before marrying Sally's father. She always spoke of that man as the one that got away. Was I to be the one she dated before she got married? The one that got away…

I told her that I couldn't live with her and I moved out. The relationship crumbled after that. The last time I saw her was the day I drove her to the airport. She moved to Germany to work as a nanny for a family friend and never came back. I started working at the bank and now I have a tumour.

In April of this year I began to have headaches. I will stress that I have lived a clean(ish) life up to this point so it was very out of the ordinary for me to have headaches at all. I never really used pain medication and had only really experienced pain so intense once before.

When I was nineteen or twenty I never used to clean inside my ears properly. The wax would build up in there and one day I guess it solidified. I can only imagine how this worked over time but something changed one day, it must have shifted or something, and it was poking me in the most painful way. I literally dropped to the floor in anguish. I went straight to a doctor and sat patiently with fears of a spider bite or that my eardrum had burst. My hearing had been somewhat affected too and I was constantly tipping my head and hoping my ears would pop and fix the problem. When I went in to see the doctor he flushed my ears with water. This process involves a long metal tray and a kind of syringe that blasts wave after wave of water into your ear. The idea is to dislodge the hard wax and have it land in the tray. It is a strange sensation. I remember looking at the tiny ball of wax in the tray and wondering how it was so painful moments ago. The human body is so fragile. Or maybe I have an incredibly bad threshold for pain. I shudder at the thought of treading on a rusty nail or having sharp shards of bamboo shoved under my fingernails.

I did something two days ago that I never thought I would do. I wrote a will. I never thought about this before now and compiling my life into possessions was extremely depressing. I'll be giving most of it away to charity.

It doesn't matter really does it?

It's all just *stuff.*

It clutters your place and distracts you from what's to come. The inevitable death that you and I and everyone we know will eventually face.

I have been thinking of telling everyone what I know. Up to now I have been the only one with the knowledge of my impending doom. I have thought about what it would be like to call my friends, one by one and tell them I'm dying. I think about the grief and sobbing. I think about having a living funeral where people can tell me what they think of me while I'm still alive.

Do I want that?

What if no one wants to come? The worst thing would be telling Sally. I picture her with two kids and a house.

A perfect husband. A perfect life.

Maybe she is unhappy. Maybe she died years ago. I'll never know unless I have a living funeral and call her. I don't really have another reason to get in touch.

Would she even want to see me?

I'd probably have to hire someone to find her.

I think I would have liked having children. Sally and I had a scare once but it turned out to be nothing. I wasn't ready then. I guess neither of us figured it would be our last chance to have a child. We really were in love though. I know that now. In retrospect the child might have resented us both. Maybe Sally would have moved away and taken our child with her.

Imagine that.

Knowing that there is a small person sharing your DNA who doesn't get the chance to meet you or know you. She could have filled our baby's head with stories about me. I would never be able to defend myself. I can imagine my children. I have such hope for them. They don't exist yet but after I'm gone they might.

I should explain.

A couple of months ago I donated sperm to several sperm banks. Besides the tumour I'm not an unfit man. I was honest and charming in my donor profile and I think one day I will give someone my ultimate gift. I will change their life forever. Maybe in the future there will be no men and only women. Then women will have to use sperm like mine to get pregnant.

Or maybe the facility where all the sperm is being kept will catch fire somehow and my donation will be lost. You can never know the future I suppose. Maybe Sally will one day choose from a long list of men and read something in my profile that triggers a memory. I guess I was feeling playful when I walked into the sperm bank and that might just come across in my profile. Maybe Sally and I *will* have a child one day. Maybe she will know it's mine somehow. It will have my eyes and she will know it or sense it.

Wishful thinking I know.

I'm a man who loved life – even though I didn't know it at the time. I never harmed people or was intentionally bad. I tried my best; probably not at the things I ought to have been trying at. I fell in love – for which I'm truly thankful. I had fun, I had friends, and I had stuff.

I can't sum it up.

It's impossible to write everything in here. I don't want to limit who I was to a paragraph and that be it.

I'm more than I could ever put down on paper. I guess I will just try and write what I can and let those who read this be the judge.

I want to live on. If I have kids I get to live on. It's so simple isn't it? My children are part of me. It's comforting to think about. No matter what, a part of me is out there. Frozen. Until someone needs it. I wish that I lived in a time where medicine had advanced so much that I could be hooked up to a computer and live on. I wish this tumour could be safely removed without causing brain damage or death.

Immortality.

Isn't that why anyone does anything? Humans are cursed with knowing that one day their time will be up. Everything else is to distract us so that we don't have mass panic, riots and hysteria. People only think about death when they get old or are faced with an insurmountable medical problem. All the songs I have ever listened to, all the films I have seen are all to distract me and entertain me *just enough*. Just enough to not wonder when my time will be up.

I guess my point is – I want to live forever. I've realised that I want to be remembered. That's why I went to the sperm bank. There must be a reason sex leads to procreation. People will always want to have sex. I have had some fantastic sexual experiences. Humans have been designed so perfectly by God or evolution or however I came to get here. If there were a God I would do any deal with him to get rid of this tumour. Or her.

I feel strange re-reading this. In a way I want to edit what I say and kind of censor my life. But then on the other hand this is kind of a final testament to who I was and something to leave behind. I want it to be as in depth as possible so I need it to have each and every thought I have before the end. If I go off on tangents or tell my story in a roundabout way then I apologise. This is the only way I know how. As I said at the beginning of this book – I'm not a writer.

This is my life.

The first time I drove a car was with my cousin. Or I suppose more accurately my cousin's boyfriend. I went on an interstate trip and slept at my uncle and aunt's place. My cousin Hilary was dating this guy with a sporty car at the time and my uncle didn't approve. He was very flashy with his money and I'm sure he seemed much richer than he actually was. I can't remember what type of car it was but it was black and very low to the ground. The inside was a cream colour that felt nice to the touch. In the town all the roads were very straight and uninteresting. There were also very wide lanes so I guess when my cousin suggested I 'drive a little' I was easily persuaded. I had no idea *how* to drive of course but the idea of learning in this amazing car was too good to pass up. I was a few months off getting my learner's licence at this stage.

We went to a car park and I remember being so thrilled when I didn't stall the car. I quickly learned from Hilary's laughter that it's not possible to stall an automatic. I did several very slow laps of the car park and was totally hooked. When I got back home I spent my savings on my first car. I bought it from my friend's dad who sold it to me for a grand. I didn't have it checked out or anything. I had to get new tyres and brake pads right away. When I asked my friend's dad about it he acted like he had no idea anything was wrong with it. He told me he had already spent my money. Since I was a kid I guess I believed him.

When the car was roadworthy I still didn't have a licence. So late at night when everyone was asleep I would drive it down to the service station and back. This would mean I had to sneak out of the house, release the handbrake and roll my car on to the road before I could start my engine. I often sped away wondering whether I had woken anyone up but I was never caught.

That was the first time I ever broke the law. I would do that same drive about three times a week late at night. Then one night I saw multiple police cars one after the other. I think their shifts must have ended around midnight because I did live near a police station. I changed my route and practiced driving. I became comfortable with my car. How mundane is my life that the thrill of *driving* has to be chronicled?

I think I really grew up during those months though. I think I started to notice girls more. Maybe they noticed me too. One girl asked me whether I shaved my forearms because they seemed so smooth. It was the weirdest thing anyone had ever said to me. Then she brushed my arm. At the time I had no idea that this was her way of flirting with me. I should have known ANY female touching you EVER is flirting. Unless they are hitting you. No – even then! I answered that I didn't shave my arms and shut her down completely. It wasn't until years later that I figured out what we were really talking about.

After I passed my driving test - and people noticed I had a car - things changed for me at school. Not in the way I had expected. I thought when I got my licence I would be giving girls rides, taking them on dates and parking with them. Instead I became socially outcast because my core group of friends still took the bus. I guess I wasn't as approachable as I thought because nobody asked me for a ride.

I have a box of photographs in front of me.

It's a strange feeling to look at pictures from your childhood and not remember them. When I look at the child in the pictures it feels like someone else's life.

One memory that comes back to me is the smell of Christmas

trees. Every Christmas the smell of a real tree would transport me to my childhood. Then we started getting plastic trees.

It's not the same. I wonder if the reason we take pictures at all is to prove we existed. Since cavemen were drawing on walls maybe it's built into our consciousness. We do it without even thinking now. I could show you a picture of my dead grandmother but that doesn't prove she lived. You'll never know her or hear her voice. You won't remember her because you never met her. After I'm gone that's how it will be for me. Just like my grandmother doesn't matter to you - I won't matter. I'm not leaving much behind either. I figured that out when I got my affairs in order.

My life didn't weigh much.

Maybe that's the point of this book. Maybe I can title it *'Don't do what I did and do nothing. Do something with your life.'*

It's a bit wordy I think.

Maybe I've wasted my time after all.

'Mr Perkins?'

I sit up.

'Markus Perkins can you hear me?'

'Y-Yes…' I manage to respond.

Before me sits a woman with straight grey hair. From her face I can tell that she is only in her twenties, making the hair a fashion choice presumably. She is wearing plain light blue scrubs. *Am I in a hospital?*

'My name is Gloria and I am a Nurse here. Are you thirsty?'

I find I am extremely thirsty so I nod.

'Mr Perkins this is going to sound like an odd line of questioning but I need to ask it. First of all, how old are you?'

'Thirty-nine.'

'And what is your profession?' she asks as she writes something down just beyond my eye line.

'I work in a bank. At least I used to.'

'Used to?'

'Before I got the tumour.'

She smiles quickly and starts writing again. She seems nervous which in turn makes me nervous.

'Someone will be with you in a moment.'

The room is white and sterile. I must have undergone some kind of medical procedure. Maybe I collapsed and was brought here. There are tubes swimming around my arms. I sense a catheter as well.

Without knocking a bearded man in a white coat bursts into the room.

'Hello Mr Perkins I'm Oliver Thompson and I'm one of the senior medical practitioners here.'

'Hello Doctor,' I say as I try to get comfortable.

'May I call you Markus?'

'Yes.'

'Markus, this will be hard to understand at first but I must tell you some things.'

'Okay...'

Oliver hands me a mirror and I look into it.

'You are not thirty-nine years old. You are also not a banker.'

'What are you talking about?'

'Markus...you have just participated in a process where we implant memories into your brain and simulate scenarios.'

'You *simulate* scenarios? What does that mean?'

'You don't have a tumour – at least not at this time. I can't guarantee that you will *never* have a tumour but you are not about to die from one. We simulated the concept that you were at death's door.'

'Why would you do that?' I ask.

'This was done at your request. Your memory will settle in time. You are actually only thirty-five years old and you have only been with us here in this facility for approximately fourteen hours.'

'And...I'm not dying?'

'No.'

'Then why would I want to…*simulate*…that I was?'

'It's true, most of our participants ask for scenarios where they're able to fulfil sexual fantasies and know what it is like to be powerful or famous. You – Markus Perkins – are already a very powerful individual. You are the CEO of this very company. I believe that you may have enjoyed such pleasant scenarios in the past but today is your birthday. Happy Birthday sir. You requested this specific scenario today. It's slightly morbid but my notes tell me that you wanted to examine your life in order to know conclusively what you wanted to do next.'

It's a lot to take in.

'It felt real. I really thought I was dying.'

'Well the technology is cutting edge. In truth you have yourself to thank sir.'

I chose to do this to myself. I'm punishing myself.

'Sally.'

'Who is Sally?' he asks me with a perplexed look.

'She's what's missing. I think she's why I did this.'

Oliver gives a short shrug.

'Well that's good. I suppose that this experiment has been a success. You will be back to your old self within the next few hours. I recommend maintaining your fluid intake and eating something when Gloria comes back in. She'll get you whatever you want.'

'What I want…is a phone.'

'Of course sir.'

He leaves the room and returns with what must be my mobile phone. I scroll through my contacts and find Sally's number.

I've had it all along.

I dial.

'Sally? It's Markus.

Did you find the number twelve in each story?

If you enjoyed these short stories
please leave a review on Amazon.

Become a fan of Twelve on Facebook
www.Facebook.com/TwelveBook

This book is also available as an Audiobook.

And keep an eye out for *Twelve More*
Coming Soon from David Farrell

About the Author

David Farrell lives in Melbourne with his wife and children.

He has Directed two independent feature films and has a film Podcast called Pod Me If You Can.

His stories *The Last Resort* & *The Glove* are available on Amazon.

His children's story *You Can't Get Rid of Me That Easily*

is also available now.

You can contact him @DaveFarrell1 on Twitter